D0864743

THE STALKER

DISCARD

Books by Bill Pronzini

Snowbound
With an Extreme Burning
Panic
Games
The Jade Figurine
Dead Run
Night Screams
Masques
The Hangings
Firewind
The Last Days of Horse-Shy Halloran
Quincannon

THE STALKER

Bill Pronzini

THE STALKER

Bill Pronzini

SPEAKING VOLUMES, LLC
NAPLES, FLORIDA
2011

THE STALKER

Copyright © 1971 by Bill Pronzini

All rights reserved. No part of this book may be reproduced or transmitted in any form or by any means without written permission of the author.

ISBN 978-1-61232-103-5

THE STALKER

The sins ye do by two and two ye must pay for one by one.

Rudyard Kipling

Tomlinson

Prologue

March, 1959

The khaki-colored Smithfield armored car entered the enclosed grounds of Mannerling Chemical, a few miles south of Granite City, Illinois, at ten minutes past nine of a cold, crisp Wednesday morning—precisely on schedule for its quarterly pick-up of the company's substantial cash receipts. It pulled to a stop in front of the Accounting Office, which was located in a wing of Building Four just inside the eastern gate, and driver Felix Marik stepped out into the frosty air to unlock the rear doors. Guards Walter Macklin and Lloyd Fosbury emerged with several empty canvas money sacks, and entered the Accounting Office.

Just as driver Marik stepped around to the side of the car, two young men dressed in dark business suits and dark overcoats, carrying small brown briefcases, approached him at a leisurely pace. They had left Parking Lot 2, directly across the asphalt roadway from Building Four, immediately after the armored car's arrival. The more muscular of the two men wore a thin black mustache attached with spirit gum, and had cotton balls inside his mouth to make his cheeks seem round and puffy; pinned to the left breast pocket of his coat was a counterfeit of the blue and white triangular identity badge which Mannerling required for admittance to its grounds. Black lettering on it read: ROBERTS, M. R.—ACCT. 4. His name was Steve Kilduff. The lean, spare man with him—wearing a set of false, bucked front teeth and whitish actor's make-up to make his normally weathered complexion seem pallid—had an identity badge which said he was Garfield, D. L., also Acct. 4. His real name was Jim Conradin.

Kilduff smiled cheerfully as they approached the Smithfield driver. He stopped and said, "Good morning."

"Morning," Marik answered.

"Little nippy out, eh?"

"You can say that again."

"Hell, what it *really* is, is ass-freezing weather."

Marik grinned. "Amen, brother."

Conradin had moved to stand next to the left front fender of the armored car. While Kilduff joked pleasantly with Marik about the weather, Jim took his slightly trembling and gloved left hand from his overcoat pocket and placed a small blob of putty-like material on the upper treads of the tire. He stepped away and nodded almost imperceptibly as Kilduff glanced at him.

Kilduff rubbed his hands together briskly. "What say we get some coffee before we go to work, Dave?"

"Good idea," Conradin said. He was trying to control a nervous tic which had gotten up along the left side of his jaw.

Marik said to them, "Well, take it slow."

"Sure," Kilduff told him. "You, too."

They moved away, passing the door to the Accounting Office. Just as they did, the door opened and Macklin and Fosbury came out with their guns drawn, each carrying several of the now-full money sacks. Kilduff and Conradin did not look at them as they re-entered the rear of the armored car. Marik locked the doors and returned to the cab and swung the car into a U-turn, heading toward the eastern gate.

Kilduff and Conradin cut diagonally across the asphalt roadway and walked slowly toward the far end of Parking Lot 2—where a six-year-old DeSoto sedan waited for them.

Kilduff said, "Clockwork, Jim."

"Yeah."

"Listen, are you all right?"

"Sure. I'm fine."

They were nearing the DeSoto now, and Conradin began to walk a little faster, his eyes fixed on the dew-streaked black hood. He was two steps in front of Kilduff, fifty feet from the sedan, when an olive-uniformed Mannerling ground-security guard, Leo Helgerman, stepped out from between two other parked cars almost directly in front of them.

Conradin stopped abruptly, and he and Helgerman stood looking at one another for a brief second—Helgerman with eyes that were faintly quizzical; Conradin's eyes round and moist with fear. Kilduff stepped around on Conradin's left, smiling disarmingly, building amiable words of greeting in his throat.

But Conradin was already moving by then, moving forward, and he brought his right hand up and slashing down across the back of Helgerman's neck. The guard's eyes rolled up in his head and he fell soundlessly to the cold, wet asphalt.

Kilduff jumped forward and caught Conradin's arm and spun him around. "You stupid son of a bitch!" he said between clenched teeth. "What did you do that for?"

Conradin stood trembling. There was a thin, silvery sheen of sweat on his face. "I don't know," he said. "I don't know."

Kilduff looked at Helgerman and saw that he was still breathing. He pulled Conradin toward the DeSoto, opened the passenger door, and shoved him inside. He went around and slid in under the wheel. The starter made a labored whirring sound, took hold, and Kilduff let out the clutch; he turned onto the company road which led to the western gate.

Conradin sat with his hands clenching his knees, and the sweat streamed down into the collar of his white shirt, smearing some of the make-up on his face and neck. He was still trembling.

"Snap out of it, will you?" Kilduff told him grimly. "Do you want to blow the whole thing?"

"Jesus," Conradin said. He was staring straight ahead. "Oh Jesus, Jesus."

But they had no trouble at the gate . . .

The stolen yellow tow truck, with the words "Dave's Garage" in blue letters on the body, was parked in a clump of willow and buckeye trees—just off the three-hundred-yard paved access road which wound through grassy fields to connect the eastern gate of Mannerling Chemical with State Highway 64.

Three men sat waiting in the cab, each of them dressed in gray work coveralls. The driver, whose name was Gene Beauchamp, said, "What if the goddamn tire doesn't blow when it's supposed to?"

"It'll blow, don't worry," the man in the middle said. He was Larry Drexel. "We tested the corrosive a dozen times, didn't we?"

"At least that."

"Okay," Drexel said. He looked at his wristwatch. "They should be coming out of the gate right about now. Let's get set."

They took grotesquely designed Hallowe'en masks from the pockets of their coveralls, slipped them over their heads, and put on peaked-bill caps pulled low. Drexel and the third man, Paul Wykopf, took blued-steel revolvers from under the seat and held them in their laps.

Drexel said, "All right. Kick it over, Gene."

Beauchamp switched on the ignition, and there was a quiet rumbling from beneath the hood. He moistened his lips. "Do you figure everything went okay?" he asked Drexel.

"Sure it did."

"I just hope there wasn't any trouble."

"Christ, will you shut up?" Wykopf said. "Kilduff knows his end of it, and so does Conradin."

"Look, I'm nervous, that's all."

"We're all nervous," Drexel said. "Cool it, now."

Wykopf hunched forward, peering through the leafy branches of one of the willow trees. "Here it comes."

The armored car was almost halfway along the access road, less than fifty yards from where they were. Drexel's hand worked spasmodically around the revolver's grip. "Blow, baby," he said softly. "Come on, baby, blow."

And the car's left front tire blew.

The heavy vehicle lurched to the side of the road, swaying as the driver fought for control, and finally shuddered to a stop. The door opened, and Felix Marik stepped out and went to inspect the damage, shouting something to the guards inside.

Drexel said, "Go!"

Beauchamp brought the tow truck out from its concealment and to a skidding halt, nose in to the armored car. Wykopf and Drexel were out and crouched ready, their guns held low and in close to their bodies, before the tow truck had ceased rocking. Marik whirled, his hand dropping toward the service pistol holstered at his side, but Drexel took two steps forward and put the muzzle of the revolver in his stomach. Marik's hand froze in midair, and Drexel took the pistol and put it into the pocket of his coveralls.

He said in a cold, sharp voice, "If you want to live to see your family again, you get the guards out of there without their guns. Now, baby!"

Beauchamp swung down from the tow truck as Drexel and Wykopf pushed Marik toward the rear of the armored car. He had several small white flour sacks strung over his left arm.

From inside the car Lloyd Fosbury said, "Felix? What in hell's going on out there?"

"Holdup," Marik said tightly. "They want you to come out unarmed."

"*What!*"

"You heard the man," Drexel said. "Now if you want your friend Felix here to keep on living, you do exactly what we tell you. You got that, baby?"

There was silence from inside, and then Fosbury said, "Yeah. We've got it."

"Unlock the doors," Drexel said to Marik.

Marik obeyed the order, using a key from his belt ring. Drexel took the ring, and then motioned Marik to one side. He called out, "The outside locks are open now. You spring the inside locks and push one of the doors open just enough to throw out your guns. All of them. I don't want to see anything come out of there but the guns."

There was the sound of movement from inside the car, and then the left door opened just a little. Drexel and Wykopf, standing off to the side, held their breaths. Two service pistols like the one Marik had worn came flashing out and fell into the grass at the rear of the truck. The door closed again.

Drexel said, "Is that all?"

"That's all," Macklin, the other guard, said.

"Now come out, one at a time, with your hands on your heads. Nice and slow."

The guards came out that way, and Drexel looked at Wykopf and nodded. "Watch them."

"They're all mine."

Drexel motioned to Beauchamp, and the two of them went inside the armored car. They began to fill the white flour sacks from the canvas money sacks. When they had all the money—something more than $750,000, although they didn't know that until later—they jumped out again, carried the flour sacks to the tow truck, and put them behind the seat. Then Drexel went back to where Wykopf was holding the three Smithfield employees.

"Into the car," he said to them, and he and Wykopf herded them inside. Drexel threw the door closed and locked it with Marik's key. He tossed the ring into the front seat of the armored car as he and Wykopf went by.

They climbed quickly into the tow truck, and Beauchamp backed the machine and got it turned around. They headed toward the entrance to State Highway 64 . . .

A half mile to the south, in a sparsely traveled area just off the Maypark Road overpass, Fred Cavalacci sat nervously waiting in a wood-paneled 1954 Chevrolet station wagon. He looked at his watch for perhaps the twentieth time in the past ten minutes, and then up at the positioned rear-view mirror.

The tow truck appeared on the overpass.

Cavalacci took the ignition key, breathing through his mouth, and got out and opened the rear door. The tow truck pulled up parallel to the wagon, and Drexel and Wykopf and Beauchamp swung out of the cab. Drexel said, "Clockwork, Fred."

Cavalacci nodded, exhaled, and drew back the heavy tarpaulin that lay on the floor of the wagon, revealing a wide rectangular space which had been hollowed out to form a pit. The four men then transferred the white flour sacks from the tow truck to the wagon. Three cars passed during the time it took them to make the switch, but none of the occupants took more than passing notice of what they assumed was a stalled motorist and the tow truck he had summoned.

When all the flour sacks were in the floor pit, Cavalacci rearranged the tarpaulin. They made sure no one was approaching in either direction, and then the four of them got inside the wagon. Cavalacci drove east, heading toward Collinsville, where they would meet Kilduff and Conradin.

They had gone almost a mile in silence when Cavalacci glanced at Drexel beside him. "We did it," he said, and there was a touch of awe in his voice. "We pulled it off."

"We did it, all right," Drexel said. He pivoted on the seat, looking at Wykopf and Beauchamp in the back. And then he began to laugh, a soft, amused, tension-releasing sound that elicited smiles, laughter from the others.

"Oh, we did it," he said, "we did it, we–did–it! And we're going to get away with it, babies! The police are never going to catch us, you mark my words!"

Larry Drexel was right.

The police never caught them . . .

October, 1970

BLUE . . .

From the Evanston, Illinois, Review, *October 3, 1970:*

BUSINESSMAN KILLED, 4 HURT IN FREAK AUTOMOBILE EXPLOSION

Elgin businessman Frederick S. Cavalacci was killed last night, and four other prominent citizens were injured, when Cavalacci's 1969 compact Chevrolet exploded in the Elks Club parking lot following an Urban Betterment League meeting.

Police sergeant Thomas Carlisle, the investigating officer, stated that there was the possibility of "fuel leakage from the carburetor somehow igniting, but we have no way of determining if this was the actual cause of the explosion." Another of the officers on the scene said that the blast was "one of those tragic things that happen sometimes, a real freak."

The other four men—David Keller, George R. Litchik, Nels Samuelson and Allan Conover—were treated for minor burns at County Memorial Hospital and subsequently released. Samuelson told reporters: "We had just come out of the meeting and were walking together toward our cars. We saw Fred get into his Camaro and heard the starter grind, and then there was this terrible, white-hot burst of flame. The concussion knocked us all off our feet. I thought the whole world had exploded."

Cavalacci, 32, owned a half-interest in Bargains, Inc.—one of Evanston's largest discount department stores. He was a native of Arden, Oklahoma, and came to this city in 1959. In 1963 he entered into partnership with Graham Isaacs of Evanston to establish Bargains, Inc. He was active in public affairs, and last year ran unsuccessfully for a seat on the City Council.

He is survived by his wife, Rona, and a seven-year-old daughter, Judith Anne.

GRAY . . .

From the Fargo, North Dakota, Forum, *October 11, 1970:*

TRUCK MISHAP CLAIMS
LIFE OF LOCAL MAN

Paul Wykopf, 34, owner of the X-Cel Trucking Company of Fargo, was crushed to death shortly past 7 p.m. last night in the company's truck garage at 1149 State Street. A failing hand brake on one of the General Motors diesel cabs parked in the garage was blamed for the tragedy. The vehicle apparently rolled forward after the hand brake slipped, pinning Wykopf against one of the concrete walls. Death was instantaneous, police said.

Gordon Jellicoe, head mechanic at X-Cel, discovered his employer's body when Wykopf failed to meet him as promised at a local tavern, and he returned to find out why. He said that Wykopf was in the habit of working late on the company books three nights each week, and that he always made a check of the premises before leaving on those evenings. "That's when it must have happened," he told police.

Wykopf was graduated from Fargo High School in 1953, where he received statewide prominence in both football and baseball. He purchased X-Cel Trucking, then called Martin's Freight Lines, from Pete Martin in 1962. The company specialized in the hauling of perishable goods.

There are no survivors.

RED . . .

From the Philadelphia Inquirer, *October 20, 1970:*

EUGENE BEAUCHAMP DIES
IN PRIVATE PLANE CRASH

Eugene Beauchamp, the wealthy Philadelphia jet-setter who last month took his third bride, steel heiress Gloria Mayes Tanner, was killed yesterday in the crash of his private plane near Lake Wallenpaupack.

Investigating officers responding to the report of a midair explosion by rancher Neil Simmons, found the smoking wreckage of the 35-year-old financial wizard's Cessna in a fallow field on Simmons' property three miles from the lake. Beauchamp was alone in the twin-engine craft at the time of the fatal plunge.

He had taken off from Kirin Field in Philadelphia early yesterday morning on a planned flight to Winnipeg, Manitoba, Canada, where he was to meet friends for a caribou-hunting expedition. He was in the habit of flying alone, a source close to the family said.

Police could find no explanation for the apparent explosion of the aircraft. A complete investigation is being conducted by the Federal Aviation Administration.

Beauchamp, whose uncanny knowledge of the stock market resulted in the accumulation of a fortune reported to exceed twenty million dollars, had devoted his time to world travel in the past few years. He was a well-known member of the fabled international jet set, and maintained homes in Côte d'Azur and on the island of Majorca, as well as in Philadelphia.

Before wedding Miss Tanner in a lavish ceremony in fashionable Beacon Hill in September, Beauchamp's name had been romantically linked with two international film starlets. His previous wives were Kelly Drew Beauchamp, an airline stewardess, and the socially prominent Marla Todd Andrews. Both marriages ended in divorce, the first in 1963 and the second in 1966.

Yellow
November 1970
Saturday and Sunday

1

Andrea was gone.

Steve Kilduff knew that, intuitively, the moment he entered their apartment high on San Francisco's Twin Peaks. He stood just inside the door, the cashmere overcoat he had shed in the elevator over his left arm, his eyes moving slowly over the neat, darkened living room—the magazines on the coffee table arranged just so, the freshly pressed drapes drawn carefully over the wide window-doors, the fireplace hearth swept clean and its steel screen placed with precise orderliness before the grate, the buff-colored shag carpet fluffy and well vacuumed, the expensive and ornate maple furnishings glistening with lemon-scented furniture polish. Everything was in its place, everything was spotlessly clean, everything was just as it always was, just as Andrea—warm, sweet, passionate, orderly Andrea—insisted it should be.

But she was gone. There was a tangible feel of desertion, of emptiness, which lay on the air in that very tidy living room like stagnating water at the bottom of a forest pool.

Kilduff shut the door quietly behind him, letting the overcoat fall to the carpet at his feet. Mechanically, he walked past the gleaming kitchen with its waxed linoleum floor and followed the short hallway into their bedroom. He saw, without seeing, that the wide double bed was neatly made, the white chenille spread free of even a single wrinkle, hanging exactly the same distance from the buff carpet on either side; that the toilet articles and jewelry cases on his dresser were schematically apportioned; that the hammered bronze ashtray on his nightstand sparkled with a recent application of tarnish remover.

He went to the walk-in closet to the left of the doorway and slid back the paneled door on Andrea's half. He looked at a bare, scrubbed wall and two dozen empty hangers uniformly bunched on the round wooden rod. The floor was equally bare; there were no pumps or heels or puff-ball slippers in the wire shoe rack, and the matching pieces of Samsonite luggage he had given Andrea for an anniversary present three years before were not there.

Kilduff returned to the living room. She hadn't even bothered to leave a note, he thought, all the conspicuous surfaces where one might have been were barren; no note, no explanation or good-bye or kiss-my-ass or go-to-hell, nothing, nothing at all.

He crossed to the closed drapes, drew them open, and unlocked the sliding glass window-doors. He stepped out onto the wide cement floor of the balcony—bare, save for the webbed aluminum summer furniture folded and stacked in one corner. A wind laced with ice particles numbed his face and neck almost immediately, but he stood with his hands on the cold metal of the welded iron railing.

The fog was coming in. It sat off to the west in great folding gray billows, like tainted cotton candy at a carnival. Kilduff watched it for a long moment—moving closer, inexorably closer, an advancing army with ephemeral wisps drifting ahead of it like the spirits of long-dead and long-forgotten generals. He moved his eyes slowly to look at what lay spread out before him: the gray close-set buildings of a big city, some hillside-clinging, some extending in long identical rows as if they had spewn forth from a gigantic duplicating machine, some jutting skyward with long, thin, beseeching spires; straight ahead to the Golden Gate Bridge, heavy with weekend traffic, the crests of its red spans already consumed by the approaching fog; across to Marin County and the brown and white and pastel cottages clinging to the side of the hill above Sausalito, where the would-be artists and the would-be writers and the hippies and the rebels and the fruiters lived; dipping lower, coming back to the ugly dead gray rock of Alcatraz, a toad's wart in the leaden surface of the bay; to the right and the cantilever span of the Bay Bridge and along it, halfway to Oakland and the East Bay, where it touches Yerba Buena Island; down and over to the naval base on the long finger, obscene finger, of Treasure Island. A sweeping panorama, Kilduff thought, beautiful San Francisco, enchanting San Francisco, but only when the sun shines, baby, because when you saw it like this, on an overcast Saturday morning in early November with the vague promise of rain and the chill of winter and the smell of acrid brine in the air, when you saw it like this it was lonely and remote and hoary-old and not very beautiful or enchanting at all.

He turned from the railing, then, and went back inside the apartment, relocking the window-doors and drawing the drapes closed again. He sank wearily onto the pliant cushions of one of the chairs and fumbled a cigarette from the pocket of his shirt. He was a big man, tall, muscular; at thirty-two, his belly was still washboard-taut and he still moved with the easy, natural grace of his youth. But his thick black hair had begun to gray prematurely at the temples, and his green and brown hawk's eyes had an almost imperceptible dullness to them, as if the fires which had once burned there were now little more than rapidly cooling embers; his cheeks were sunken hollowly, giving him an anomalous, slightly satanic look. It was a strange face that stared back at him from the mirror in the bathroom every morning, a face he no longer felt at ease with after eight years of almost-but-not-quite, eight years of failure compounded upon failure, eight years of knowing that the money would run out some day and trying to look ahead to that time, trying to prepare for it in advance, and never accomplishing that objective—or any other.

Like these past two days, he thought. Like what had happened with this Roy Bannerman, whom he had met at an incredibly sluggish party some friends of Andrea's had given on Russian Hill. Bannerman was an executive with a large independent cannery in Monterey, and there was a managerial position opening up there shortly that paid twelve thousand per annum. Come on down, he had told Kilduff, I'll have the brass over for dinner, give them a chance to look you over; hell, a few drinks and some thick steaks under their belts, and you're in, Steve, I can practically guarantee it. So he had gone down there and met the brass, putting the charm on, smiling at the right time, laughing at the right time, speaking at the right time, lying at the right time, oh Jesus yes, he had impressed the crap out of them, they were calling him Steve and he was calling them Ned and Charley and Forry, and when the evening was over they had said to come around to the cannery in the morning and take a tour of the plant, see what you'll be handling, eh, Steve, and he had called Andrea from his motel bursting like a goddamned kid with a straight-A report card. She had sounded pleased, in a subdued way, strange now that he thought of it, but he had put it down at the time to the late hour and the fact that he had gotten her out of bed. So he had gone around to the cannery yesterday, Friday, and a fat secretary with bad legs had taken his name and then informed him that Ned and Charley and Forry were all in conference, would he mind waiting for just a little while? He waited for three hours, and then Bannerman came into the anteroom looking very righteous, and said that it had all fallen through, they had run a personnel check into his background as a matter of policy and what the hell, Steve, why didn't you tell me about all those screw-ups before I went through the trouble of setting everything up, we've got to have a solid man in this position, somebody who can step right in and take over, well, I hope you understand.

He understood; he understood all too well.

But it didn't really matter now, because the money had finally run out—there was exactly three hundred and sixteen dollars in their joint checking account—and because Andrea had run out, too.

Andrea, he thought. He stared blankly through the smoke curling upward from his cigarette. Andrea, why? *Why?* We had something, didn't we? We had it all, didn't we? We had a love that transcended all the failures, all the empty purposes, enduring, unshakable, unkillable, a veritable Rock of Gibraltar . . .

Bullshit.

It was the money, of course.

Face the truth, Kilduff—no more money, no more Andrea; simple enough, painfully simple enough. He should have seen that, even though they had never discussed the money by tacit agreement; he had told her in the beginning that it was an inheritance from a non-existent granduncle Andrew in Cedar Rapids, Iowa, and she had accepted that. That was where he had made his mistake, taking her unquestioning acceptance of the money and her silence on the subject to mean that it carried no real import for her. But all the time she had been waiting, biding her time, squeezing all but the very last little drop.

And then: Good-bye, Steve. *In absentia.* It was nice while the money lasted.

Bodega Bay is a small fishing village on the Northern California coast, some sixty-five miles above San Francisco. The village, the good-sized inlet of the same name, and a complex of several buildings called The Tides, achieved a kind of national prominence some years ago when Alfred Hitchcock filmed his suspense movie *The Birds* there. Since that time, they get a good percentage of tourist business in the spring and summer months—sightseers, vacationers, visitors from outlying towns, self-styled fishermen who boast to the bored party-boat captains about the record king salmon they are going to land but never do. But during the winter, the natives usually have the place pretty much to themselves, and it takes on—falsely—the atmosphere of one of those staid, aloof New England-seacoast hamlets.

At The Tides, inside the Wharf Bar and Restaurant, Jim Conradin sat in solitary silence at the short bar, drinking two fingers of bourbon from a water glass. All of the burnished copper-topped tables in the coffee shop area were empty. Sal, the bartender, was having an animated discussion with the lone waitress, a young girl named Dolly, with hair the color of wheat sheaves and very large breasts which Sal watched hungrily as he spoke. There was no one else present.

Conradin, dressed in a sheepskin jacket and blue denim trousers, turned on his stool to look out through the windows with deep-set, brooding gray eyes. The chiseled, weather-bronzed features of his lean face were grim. A storm was building somewhere out at sea—a day, perhaps two, away; the vague smell of dark rain had been in the air when he arrived at The Tides some two hours earlier. The bay was rough, an oily grayish-black color; whitecaps covered its surface, causing the red-and-white buoys that marked the crossing channel to bob and weave violently, and three or four high-masted fishing boats anchored downwind to rock heavily in the swells. He couldn't see much of Bodega Head, across the bay, and the narrows that led into the Pacific at the southern end was completely obliterated by swirling fog. Old man Rushing, who had been a sailing master once and had come around Cape Horn in a two-masted schooner in 1923, sat dressed in his perennial faded blue mackinaw and leather deer-hunter's cap on the edge of the wooden dock, fishing for crappies with a hand line, impervious to the cold and the fog and the wind. It seemed to Conradin, as it always did when he saw him, that the old man had been built, too, when they constructed the dock.

Conradin turned back to his bourbon, staring moodily into the glass. He hated winter, hated it with consummate vehemence. It was a sedentary time, a time of waiting, a time of thinking. God, that was the worst part—the thinking. When the salmon were running, it was a different story altogether. Then you could stand on the solid hardwood deck of your boat in a three-mile-per-hour troll, with the warm sea breeze fresh and heady in your nostrils and the sound of the big Gray Marine loud and vibrant in your ears; you could feel in your hands the power, the resiliency of a thirty-pound hickory-butted Harnell rod with a 4/0 reel and a fifty-pound monofilament test line; you could see the big silvers close out on the green-glass ocean, coming out of the water in long graceful jumps to rid themselves of sea lice, the way marlin will do to shake the sucking fish from their gills; you could watch them, feel them hit the Gibbs-Stewart spoons or the live sardines, whichever you were using, leaping end over end and then turning and running toward the boat, broad tails lashing the water to foam, then sounding to take the line out again; you could play them, fight them, pit raw stamina against raw stamina, know the exhilaration of landing them, of winning, of taking them with their shining bluish-silver bellies onto the ice. There was no time for thinking, then, no time for dwelling on a past that refuses to stay buried. But in the winter . . .

Conradin drained the balance of the amber fluid. He debated having another drink; he had had four already, and he could feel them just a little. It was barely noon, and Trina would have lunch for him before long, in the big white house overlooking the bay from the northern flat. Still, there was time for one more; there was always time for one more.

He glanced toward Sal, the bartender, who now had his face very close to Dolly's, whispering something in her ear. She giggled girlishly, her face reddening. Conradin said, "How about a refill."

Grudgingly, Sal moved away from the girl to pour two more fingers of bourbon into the empty glass. When he took Conradin's dollar, his eyes said that anybody who drank ten fingers of sour mash before noon was a goddamned lush, or something.

Trina might have agreed with that, in a way; Trina said he drank too much, and maybe she was right. But only in the winter, he thought, only when there was the time for thinking.

Silently, he raised the glass to his lips.

When Larry Drexel brought his sleek jade-green Porsche 912 SL to a stop in the driveway of his tile-roofed hacienda-style home in Los Gatos, he saw that Fran Varner was waiting for him on the rear patio. She was propped up on one of the chaise longues near the stone fountain in the patio's center, reading a paperback book. A bulky-knit sweater was draped over her shoulders, and the short sky-blue skirt she wore had hiked up to expose her slender legs to a pale November sun which danced intermittently behind heavy clouds. Her rich seal-brown hair was carefully combed, curved under at the nape of her neck, the way he liked her to wear it.

Drexel smiled a little as he set the parking brake, thinking that if he had somehow been crazy enough to marry her, as she had been after him for six months to do, then she would be greeting him when he came home from El Peyote—wrapped in a shapeless housecoat, with her hair up in rollers. This way, with the arrangement, she was always at her best for him—even when they were in bed, especially then, putting that cream sachet he liked in all the secret little places and sleeping in the nude instead of in the old flannel nightgown he knew she wore at her apartment.

Dark-haired and dark-complected, looking somewhat like the actor Ricardo Montalban though he was not of Latin descent, Drexel stepped onto the flagstone walk that paralleled the house. He moved with almost feline fluidity inside his two-hundred-dollar sharkskin suit, following the path past the bottle brush and barrel cactus in the landscaped borders. When he reached the patio, his eyes—black, expressive, sharply watchful—moved approvingly over the rows of *macetas* with their potted desert plants, the four asymmetrical Joshua trees like miniature Briareuses, the six-foot stone and mortar wall separating the patio from the narrow creek that wound its way past the rear of his property. It had an Old-Mexico feel which never failed to please him; he had a thing about Mexican-Spanish architecture and motif.

Fran stood as he approached, smoothing her skirt and touching her hair with that almost self-conscious movement women seem to affect. "Hi, honey," she said, kissing him.

He held her for a moment, his hand moving in a familiar way along the gentle curve of her hip. "A little cool for the patio, isn't it?"

"Well, it got to be stuffy inside."

"Been waiting long?"

"Since noon."

"Any mail?"

"A couple of things," she said. "I put them on the hall table." She slipped her arm about his waist. "Have you eaten lunch yet? It's past one."

"Juano brought me a sandwich," Drexel said. "Listen, Fran, you're going to have to work half a day tomorrow, noon till five. Elena's brother is getting married in Watsonville."

"Okay." She sighed wistfully. "It must be a lovely feeling to know you're about to become a bride or a groom in twenty-four hours."

"You're not going to start in again, are you?"

"No, honey. I was just thinking about Elena's brother."

"Sure," Drexel said. "Come on, let's go inside and do it on the kitchen table."

She blushed crimson, poking his arm. He grinned. This kid was something else, that was a fact. She couldn't get enough of it, Christ she wore him out sometimes, but when you came right out and talked about it in the light of day, without the sun having set and the shades having been drawn and the lamp having been put out, she acted as if she'd never before seen or heard of a hard-on. Maybe it was that blushing schoolgirl innocence that had made him keep her around as long as he had; it was like making it with a virgin every time.

They entered the house through the glass-enclosed archway off the patio, stepping into the parlor. It was dark in there, shadowed and with very little color. The furniture was old and heavy and ponderous and expensive. An imposing scrolled desk sat on one side of the room, and on the rear wall, in close proximity to one another, were a religious mural and an oblong painting of a nude girl on blue velvet; a few people had been shocked by the impact of *that* juxtaposition, Drexel thought amusedly.

He went to the hall table and retrieved his mail. There was a telephone bill, and an advertisement for some real estate development called Whispering Echoes in Southern Oregon, and a two-week-old copy of the Philadelphia *Inquirer*. He put the phone bill in a slot marked PAYABLE in the wooden back of the desk, and the advertisement in the fieldstone fireplace; he took the newspaper to a brocade couch and began to peel off the mailing wrapper.

Fran said, "Why do you take newspapers from all over the country? Have you got relatives or something in Illinois and North Dakota and Pennsylvania?"

If only you knew, sweets. But he said, "No, it's just a hobby. Some people collect stamps or coins or old rubbers. I collect newspapers."

She blushed again. "Want some coffee?"

"Fine."

She disappeared into the kitchen. Drexel lighted one of the thin black cheroots he affected, and spread the paper open. He began to scan it with practiced expertise, chuckling a little at Fran's reaction to the idea of anyone collecting old rubbers. But the smile left his face abruptly when his eyes fell on the headline in the upper left-hand corner of Page Four: EUGENE BEAUCHAMP DIES IN PRIVATE PLANE CRASH. Holy Jesus, he thought. He put out the cheroot and read the accompanying story carefully; then he refolded the paper and laid it on the cushion beside him.

He stood and began to pace the muted Navajo rug, his mind working coldly, methodically, weighing and considering.

Fran came in a moment later. "Honey, there isn't any cream. Do you want—?"

"Shut up," Drexel said without looking at her. "Shut the hell up."

"But I—"

"I told you to shut up. Get out of here. I'll call you later."

"Larry, what is it? What's the matter?"

"Damn you, do what I say!"

A mixture of hurt and confusion made liquid form at the corners of her amber-colored eyes. She stood rigidly for almost ten seconds, and then she said, "All right, then!" and ran toward the hallway that led to the front entrance. The sound of the thick, arched wooden door slamming behind her caused faint reverberations to drift through the dark house.

Drexel continued to pace, still weighing, still considering. Finally, having made a decision, he went to the scrolled desk and unlocked the bottom drawer on the right side with a key from his pocket case. Inside, there was an old ersatz-leather scrapbook and a smaller, clothbound address book. He took the address book out and opened it and studied the facing page.

After a moment, he turned and went to where the telephone sat on an oddly shaped driftwood stand near the arched patio entrance.

2

United Airlines Flight 69, non-stop from Philadelphia, arrived at San Francisco International Airport at 1:26 P.M., four minutes ahead of schedule. One of the first passengers to disembark—when the mobile exit ramp had been locked into place at the fore and aft doors—was a small, rather nondescript man who walked with a noticeable limp. He had ridden the blue-carpet coach, and had slept through a technicolor movie with Gregory Peck and the passage of the two-limit cocktail cart and the distribution of chicken cordon bleu by two blonde stewardesses with portrait smiles; but as soon as the wheels of the DC-8 had touched the approach runway, he had been instantly alert, piercing sand-colored eyes peering intently through the window on his left, fingers drumming impatiently on a thin leather American Tourister briefcase which had never left his lap.

He passed through the railed observation area at Gate 30, and moved with surprising speed for a limping man along the north wing of the terminal. Outside the glassed outer wall, fog eddied in gray waves, like mounds of steel wool, across the pattern of concrete runways—but he took little notice of it.

In the main lobby, a blue and white sign above a set of escalators read: BAGGAGE CLAIM. He rode down to the lower level and waited by the huge revolving baggage carousel which was designated by his flight number. Some of the other passengers began to arrive, and a fat woman wearing an incongruous plumed hat came over to stand beside him. She had sat across the aisle on the plane.

"This takes forever," she said in a strident voice. "You'd think the airlines would be more efficient. Things haven't changed a bit since my first flight to San Francisco in 1947. Not a bit, mind you."

The limping man glanced at her briefly, and then looked away. The first pieces of luggage began to flow out of the conveyor chute in the center of the sloping chrome carousel.

"Look at that," the fat woman said, pursing her lips and pointing one huge arm at the chute. "They come out of there so fast, they get all banged up when they hit the sides. My best overnight bag has a crease on one end because of that. Why can't they find another way to get the luggage out of the plane, some way that doesn't damage everything you own."

The limping man unwound two fingers from the handle of the briefcase and began to tap them irritably against the leather. He said nothing.

"If there's another crease in any of my bags, I'm going to demand the terminal replace it with a new one," the fat woman said. "They're responsible, after all."

A dun-colored pasteboard suitcase with a cracked plastic handle came out of the chute. It slid down to the rubberized bumper ringing the bottom sides of the carousel. When it had revolved to where he was standing, the limping man lifted it out quickly. The woman said, "You'd better examine the end of it. It probably has a crease in it, just like my—"

"Shut up, you fat ugly useless bitch," the limping man whispered softly, fervently. He turned and began to walk rapidly toward the south end of the level.

The fat woman made a surprised hennish sound deep in the folds of her throat. Spots of crimson fired her cheeks. She raised one trembling arm and pointed it after him, still making the sounds; fat jiggled on her upper arm like an inverted gelatin mold. The other passengers watched her. They had not heard the limping man's words.

A moment later, he stopped at an enclosed booth representing one of the car rental agencies. A man in an ostentatious Madras jacket smiled unctuously at him from behind the counter. "Yes, sir?"

"I want a compact Chevrolet or Ford, light-colored, quiet engine."

"Certainly, sir."

"I'll need it for a week. Ten days at the most."

"May I see some identification, please? Driver's license and any major credit card."

The limping man set the pasteboard suitcase on the floor at his feet and took his wallet from the inside pocket of his faded brown suit jacket; he did not set the briefcase down. The unctuous man studied the driver's license and an oil company credit card in the proffered wallet, nodded, and then consulted a list by his left elbow. "Would a Ford Mustang be acceptable, sir?"

"That's all right."

The unctuous man lifted a telephone, spoke briefly into it, and then rotated a pad of contract forms. The limping man filled out the single-page contract, signed it, and was given the last two pages in a card folder upon which the clerk had written the license number of the Ford Mustang and the stall where it could be located in the outside parking area.

The limping man picked up the pasteboard suitcase, went quickly to the far end of the level, and stepped through a door into the gelid afternoon.

Ice drops stung his skin and the wind whipped mercilessly at his sparse brown hair; but he seemed oblivious to the cold as he walked among the rental cars to his designated stall. A bearded boy in a white uniform with the agency's name in bright blue across the back waited there for him. The boy looked at the card folder, inclined his head, and held the door open. The limping man ignored a tip-waiting hand and slid beneath the wheel of the Mustang. The keys were in the ignition.

He proceeded through the parking area fronting the airport and entered the northbound ramp leading onto the James Lick Freeway. The speedometer needle climbed to seventy and seemed to lock there; the limping man drove with both hands competently on the steering wheel, his eyes leaving the broken white line before him only to check the side- and rear-view mirrors prior to changing lanes.

Fifteen minutes later, he bore right at the Skyway and Central Freeway junctions, following the Skyway to the Seventh Street exit. He had been in San Francisco only once previously—two months ago—but he had memorized this route, and several others, with precise care. He had been over each more than once.

At Sixth Street, he crossed Market to enter Taylor; at the corner of Taylor and Geary, he turned into a parking garage. He left the Mustang with an attendant and carried the two cases along Geary to a small, unpretentious hotel called the Graceling.

Fingers again working in metronome cadence on the surface of the briefcase, he spoke to the polite, if somewhat bored, hotel clerk and signed the register. An aging bellhop with a faintly sour smell about him responded to the clerk's summons, picked up the limping man's suitcase, and led him over to a self-service elevator at the near end of the lobby. On the fourth floor, the bellhop unlocked the door to Number 412, placed the key on the lacquered dresser inside, laid the suitcase on an aluminum luggage rack near the window, and then returned to the doorway. He stood waiting. The limping man's eyes, unblinking, met the bellhop's liquidy blue ones; after a moment, the bellhop coughed nervously, averting his gaze, and retreated into the hallway.

When he had closed and locked the door, the limping man sat on the wide double bed and opened the briefcase with a tiny key from the breast pocket of his suit. From inside, he extracted a thick ten-by-thirteen manila envelope and put it on his lap; he did not touch the heavy Ruger .44 Magnum Blackhawk revolver which lay in a chamois cloth at the bottom of the case.

Opening the manila envelope, he removed two sets of three folders each, both sets being fastened with thick, sturdy rubber bands. The folders were of the type used by college students for term paper assignments, and were of different colors. Those in one set were blue, gray, and red; those in the second were yellow, green, and orange. He glanced cursorily at the first set—blue and gray and red—and then returned it to the manila envelope. He slid the rubber band from the second set and placed its three folders side by side on the floral bedspread.

Each contained several sheets of ruled notepaper filled with lines of writing in an almost illegible backhand, and a Mobil Oil Travel and Street Map. The writing consisted of daily journal-like reports, over a two-week span, which the limping man had made on his first trip to California two months previous; they were detailed with names, numbers, dates, places, habits, and observations.

He sat staring at the names inked in large block letters on the front of each folder. Which one next? he asked himself silently. Well, it didn't really make a great deal of difference, it would all be over within the week anyway—for him, and for each of them.

At length he selected the yellow folder, lay back on the bed, and began to study its contents, even though he had long since committed to memory each fact represented there.

It wasn't the money at all.

But Steve will believe it is, Andrea Kilduff thought. Oh yes, that's exactly what he'll believe.

She drove the little tan Volkswagen carefully, allowing five car-lengths between herself and the station wagon ahead. She was just coming into San Rafael now, some twenty miles north of San Francisco, and the Saturday afternoon traffic on U.S. Highway 101 was badly congested. Andrea wished she hadn't put off leaving the city so long—what had she expected to happen, sitting there in that virtually empty café on Parnassus for more than two hours: her conscience or guardian angel or something to come and sit on the stool beside her like in those silly television commercials and talk her out of it? Well, it wouldn't be long before she reached Duckblind Slough, and she was thankful that Steve hadn't decided on Antioch or Stockton, both of which had also been under consideration that summer six years ago; driving in heavy freeway traffic always unnerved her, especially when any appreciable distance was involved.

Tiny, almost doll-like, she possessed that type of finely boned, aesthetic face which is coveted by fashion photographers and portrait painters. She felt, without vanity, that her mouth was just a little too small, her luminous black eyes under feathery natural lashes just a little too large; but each, in fact, contributed subtly yet prominently to a fragile, almost Dresden beauty. Her legs were perfectly proportioned in relation to her size, and her breasts were well defined, if rather small—she had always thought men disliked small breasts, but Steve had told her once, in bed, that the big-boob myth was just that, a myth, propagated by some Madison Avenue ad agency with a brassiere account, anything more than a mouthful was just wasted anyway. On this day, she wore a pair of tailored tweed slacks, a cardigan sweater, and a pale green silk scarf over her short ebon hair.

Watching the car ahead of her cautiously, she thought: He won't recognize the real reason I've gone. If it enters his mind at all he'll reject it, because he doesn't know, hasn't any idea, what has happened to him these past few years. And the terrible thing is, no matter what I do, he almost surely never will.

A person is able to endure just so much—emotionally as well as physically—wasn't that a true fact? Alone in the apartment last night—listening to silence, waiting for Steve to call and knowing that he hadn't gotten the cannery job, of course, that he was brooding child-like in his motel room the way he had done before—Andrea had been struck with the realization that since this was by no means the final failure, was in fact simply another link in the chain, it was also by no means the final night she would be left listening to silence, waiting for him to call or to come home with the news that still another job hadn't gone through, still another opportunity had been cast adrift on the wind. She saw herself twenty years hence, hair graying, skin already crosshatched with furrows and lines and purplish wrinkles; she saw herself without hope, dying inside by degrees—the way it had already become with Steve—and she was terrified.

Even though she still loved him deeply, the thought of watching him become less and less of a man through the coming days and months and years was inconceivable. And there was nothing she could do to prevent it; failure in the past precluded success in the future, how long could you beat your head against the proverbial stone wall without even so much as chipping the mortar? She had to leave then, quickly and quietly, like a thief in the night, without tearful good-byes, bitter good-byes, without the painful, useless explanation. Andrea knew that if she waited for Steve to come back, and came to that final confrontation, she would not be able to handle things, would not, very possibly, be able to leave at all. She had tried to write him a short note, but the right words refused to come; after five attempts, five "Steve darling" salutations, she had given it up. When she had had time to prepare herself, after a few days alone to put it all together, she would call him and tell him the simple truth—even though he wouldn't believe it. Then . . .

Well, she would have plenty of time in the next few days to consider *then.*

Shivering a little, even though the windows were tightly rolled up and the Volkswagen's heater was turned to high, and with a conscious effort of will, she gave her full concentration to driving.

It wasn't until she had gone another five miles, leaving San Rafael behind her, that Andrea felt the wetness on her cheeks and realized she was crying.

3

It was a voice out of the past, dimly remembered in that first groping effort at placement but then becoming violently, jarringly, familiar; an insinuating, phlegmatic voice saying very distinctly over a telephone wire, "Steve? Steve Kilduff?"

Standing in the hallway, between the kitchen and the bedroom, Kilduff gripped the receiver so tightly that the tendons in his wrist began to ache. The back of his neck had suddenly grown cold.

"Steve?" Drexel asked again. "Is that you?"

"Yes," he answered finally. "Hello, Larry."

"A long time, baby."

"Not long enough."

"Maybe yes, maybe no."

"Our agreement is still binding."

"Not now, it isn't."

"What makes now special?"

"I think we'd better get together, Steve."

"Why?"

"I can't go into it over the phone."

"Granite City?"

"Granite City."

"How important?"

"Damned important."

"Discovery?"

"Maybe. I'm not sure."

Dear God, Kilduff thought.

Drexel said, "But not the way you're thinking."

Steve transferred the receiver from his left hand to his right, wiping the moist palm on the leg of his trousers. There was a dry, lacquered taste in his mouth. "All right," he said slowly. "When?"

"Tonight."

"Where?"

"We'd better make it your place," Drexel said. "Can you get rid of your wife for the evening?"

"She's already gone," Kilduff said, a trace of bitterness coming into his tone. He didn't offer to elaborate. "Why does it have to be here?"

"Halfway house."

"I don't get you."

"Between Bodega Bay and Los Gatos."

"Where are you?"

"Los Gatos."

"And Bodega Bay?"

"Jim Conradin."

"Will he be here, too?"

"If I can reach him."

"What about the others?"

"No, just the three of us."

"If it's Granite City, it concerns them, too."

"Not any more, it doesn't."

"What's that supposed to mean?"

Drexel said, "Eight o'clock."

There was a soft click from the other end of the line.

Kilduff stood holding the phone for a long moment, and then, carefully, replaced it in its cradle. He returned to the living room and stood in the middle of the buff-colored carpet. Discovery? he had asked. Maybe, Drexel had said; but not the way you're thinking. What had he meant by that? Was it possible, after eleven years, eleven *years*, that somebody could have tied them to Granite City? No, that was completely inconceivable; the investigation had been dropped long ago, the Statute of Limitations had long since run its course. And even if it were somehow incredibly true, there was nothing the authorities could do, was there? Oh, they could bring it all out into the open, expose them all to the publicity, but that was really all, wasn't it? Unless they would be able to demand repayment of the money, in spite of the fact that there was no chance of actual criminal prosecution. He couldn't remember. Gene Beauchamp had been the legal expert, he had figured all the angles, all the probabilities and potentialities; he had been the one who told them that they had to remain in Illinois until the Statute ran out—three years. If you left the state during that time, and you were ever caught, you were still liable to Federal indictment for interstate flight to avoid prosecution for armed robbery.

What *about* Beauchamp? he wondered. And Cavalacci and Wykopf? Why had Drexel said it didn't concern them any more? Had something already happened, had the others somehow been taken into custody? Christ, if . . . No, no, no. If the authorities had learned of three, they would have learned of all six; if they had gotten three, they would have gotten all six. It was something else then, something else . . .

Kilduff went into the bathroom on rubbery legs and ran some cold water into the shell-pink basin and splashed it over his face and neck. He looked at himself in the medicine cabinet mirror. His face had a grayish, unhealthy cast; fear, the old fear, the trapped fear, had replaced the dullness in his eyes. He looked away, reaching mechanically for one of the velour towels on the rack next to the shower bath. Another thought came into his mind, then: How had Drexel known where to find him? How had he known he lived in San Francisco? After the Statute of Limitations had run out, and they were able to leave Illinois, they had all gone their separate ways, none of them telling the others what their plans were, what their eventual destinations were. That had been an integral part of their agreement, just as their pledge never to contact one another had been an integral part. Since Drexel lived so near him—in Los Gatos, hadn't he said? less than fifty miles away—it could be that he had somehow run across Kilduff during the past eight years. Still, the telephone was listed in Andrea's name, he had insisted upon that, and he hadn't been married, hadn't even known Andrea, in Illinois. And there was the fact, too, that Drexel knew about Jim Conradin living in Bodega Bay . . .

Kilduff's temples began to throb rhythmically, achingly, and there was the distant half-realized sound of surf in his ears. Robot-like, he went into the living room again and sat on the chair he had occupied earlier. It's all beginning to crumble, his mind said; first the money running out, and then Andrea leaving, and now Drexel coming impossibly out of the past—it's finally beginning to crumble.

He sat with his hands gripping the cushioned side of the chair, staring at the closed drapes. After a while, some of the tautness left his body and the pressure at his temples abated. He took several deep, tremulous breaths, looking up to the sunburst clock on the near wall. It was a little past two.

Six hours. He knew he couldn't sit there, waiting, alone, in the neat, empty, antiseptic apartment. He had to get out; a walk, a drive, anything, he had to get out.

Trina Conradin stood at the sitting room window, staring past the shimmering sea of vermilion and pink and lavender ice plants in the front yard. It was one of those old-fashioned, multi-paned windows, with a dome-shaped, lead stained-glass rosetta above it, and the imperfectness of the panes and the ebbing gray tendrils of fog made the retreating figure of her husband seem frighteningly surrealistic.

She watched him get into their eight-year-old Dodge, and a moment later heard the sound of the starter and a sharp, metallic rending as the automatic transmission was jerked out of neutral. The rear tires spun on the crushed-shell drive, and the car shot ahead, going too fast, its red brake lights coming on like twin demon's eyes in the fog as he slowed momentarily to negotiate the sharp turn at the bottom of the inclined drive; then the car disappeared onto Shoreline Highway, east around the curve of the northern flat of Bodega Bay, toward Highway 1.

Trina stood at the window for a long moment, and then, with her long thin hands hugging her shoulders, she turned to face the dark sitting room. There had been a time when she took pleasure in that room, in the ponderously heavy oak paneling of the walls, the tarnished-brass floor and table lamps with their tasseled shades, the dated wing chairs with their tufted velvet seats and heavy black lacquered arms that had begun to spider-web with thousands of tiny age cracks; there had been a time when the old white house, which had been built by a wealthy Irishman when the area around Bodega Bay produced great quantities of potatoes in the early 1900's, had evoked from her happy comments of "quaint" and "picturesque." But now the house, and this room, seemed only somber and somehow faintly foreboding, harboring ghosts and faded memories that were as musty as the sometimes intangible, sometimes pronounced odor which seemed to permeate the dwelling.

Slowly, Trina moved through the sitting room to the spacious hallway leading to the rear of the house. She paused there, looking at the telephone on its eagle-claw stand. She worried her lower lip, still hugging herself, thinking of the call only a few short minutes earlier—a man's voice she had never heard before, asking for Jim Conradin. She had called him out of the kitchen, where he had been eating the Crab Louis she had prepared for lunch, his face red from the whiskey she knew he had been drinking at The Tides that morning. At the sink in the kitchen, she had heard him say hello. There had been an instant of silence, and then Jim's voice, strange and breathless in her ears, saying, "Sweet Mother of God!" A short, sibilant, unintelligible conversation followed, and she was aware that he had lowered his voice to prevent her from hearing. When he came into the kitchen moments later, his face had chameleoned from red to bone-white, and his eyes were veiled.

"Jim, what is it?" she had asked, alarmed.

"I have to go out now."

"But you haven't finished your lunch."

"I don't have time for it," he had told her, pulling his sheepskin jacket off the chair back.

"Is it that important?"

"Business. Something's come up."

"Well, where are you going?"

"San Francisco."

"San Francisco? Whatever for?"

"It's nothing that concerns you."

"Jim . . ." she had begun, but he was already moving toward the front of the house, taking the car keys from the pocket of his jacket, slamming the door on his way out to cut off her words as she called after him again.

Trina passed a hand through her long dark hair, sighing tremulously now. She was thirty-one years old, with the slim, athletic figure of a girl; but the tiny crow's feet at the corners of her brownish-gold eyes, the rather stern set of a mouth that had not had occasion to smile or laugh often in the past few years, made her seem even older than her years. She sighed again, pulling Jim's old brown sweater tightly about her shoulders, and entered the kitchen. She began to clear off the table, thinking of her husband, as she always did when she was alone.

When she had first met him, when he was a senior and she a junior at Healdsburg High School in 1955, he had been such an outgoing person, fun to be with and to know, always ready to embark on some new adventure, always the first to suggest a picnic or a beach party or a hiking trip through the redwoods. She remembered the time they had driven to Mt. Lassen for the weekend, just the two of them, one summer when she was staying with her permissive Aunt Jocelyn; they had slept under the stars in two old sleeping bags he had borrowed from a friend, close together, by a stone-ringed fire in an isolated clearing, and she had known she was in love with him then because he had only kissed her once, gently, in the moonlight, and hadn't tried to take advantage of her or of the situation. She remembered the week before he left to enter the Army, when he had given her the gold band engagement ring with its thin circle of tiny diamonds, a very expensive ring that he had bought with money he'd saved from his summer job in the apple orchards near Sebastopol; and how she had said she would wait for him, wouldn't even go to a movie with another boy, and how she had been faithful to that promise. She remembered the letters, love letters—she still had them tied with a faded blue ribbon in the bottom drawer of her dresser—that he had written to her, one each week, faithfully, and the ones she had written to him. She remembered when he had called her after his discharge to say that he was going into some kind of business venture in Illinois for a while, he wouldn't tell her what it was, very hush-hush, and that he would return to California when he had saved enough money for them to be married and to buy that salmon fishing boat he had always talked about having. She remembered how she had pleaded with him to allow her to come out to Illinois, they could be married there, but he had said that the business venture would be taking up all of his time, he couldn't be with her the way a husband should, and that was no way to start a marriage; she had acquiesced, finally, and had written to him every day and he to her twice a week.

And then, three years later, he had come home with all the money he had saved—he wouldn't tell her how much, just that it was considerable and they wouldn't have to worry about anything for a long while to come—and they had been married in the little white church near her home in Healdsburg. He had bought the salmon boat and this house in Bodega Bay, and she had never been happier.

But she had begun to sense that something was wrong almost immediately. Jim had changed—in small ways at first, hardly noticeable, and then as the years passed, in progressively larger ways until he became a different man. Where he had always been outgoing, warmly laughing, making new friends, he became introverted, reticent, almost rude at times to neighbors and acquaintances; where he had always been ready to investigate new things and new places, constantly on the move, he became almost a recluse, leaving Bodega Bay only on the rarest of occasions—what was the use of having a home and a business someplace if you were going to be running around the country all the time? They had talked about children before, in their letters and when they were together, and Jim had said he wanted a large family, four boys and four girls; laughingly, "I'm going to keep you barefoot and pregnant, woman." But when Trina had suggested having a child right away, he had said he'd changed his mind, they should wait for a while longer, and it was the same answer every time she broached the subject to him. Also, there was the fact that he had begun drinking. She couldn't understand that; he had never been one for liquor, even in high school—when the other boys had gone out on weekend beer busts, he had usually begged off, or if he did go, he was the one who invariably ended up driving the others home. Now he drank heavily, almost habitually, in the winter months, when the salmon weren't running; in the summer, he put himself into the fishing with a fervor that she thought bordered on the fanatical.

Trina couldn't understand any of it. Could it have been her? She had asked herself that question an incalculable number of times, and had unfailingly given it the same answer: No. She had been everything a good wife should be, she was certain of that—she loved him, she was interested in him, in what he did and said and felt, she was passionate, trusting, undemanding. No, it wasn't her; it was something else, something, possibly, that had happened while he was in the Air Force or when he was involved in that business venture in Illinois. But she could never get him to talk about that; he always managed to change the subject when she brought it up. Perhaps that call today had had something to do with it, perhaps . . .

An involuntary shudder moved across her shoulders. She wished Jim had not gone to San Francisco, she wished that call had never come. There was something . . . something *sinister* about it—melodramatic as that sounded—something dangerous and alien and incomprehensible.

Suddenly, intuitively, Trina Conradin was more frightened than she had ever been in her life.

4

The fishing shack squatted on the very tip of a narrow point in Duckblind Slough—a subordinate tributary of the Petaluma River several miles north of where that body of water empties into San Pablo Bay, and some thirty miles north of San Francisco. One of three similar structures in the slough—the others were set inland one hundred yards on either side—it was low and box-shaped and seemed to list slightly toward the water, as if the strength of the wind had been too much for it to withstand. It was built of raw, unfinished sawmill planks, covered with tar paper for insulation purposes, and it sat raised some two feet off the thick gray-black mud of the sloping bank, on four wooden corner blocks. Attached to the rear, immediately beneath one of the shack's two windows, was a short floating dock, tar-papered like the shack itself, that jutted some fifteen feet into the turbid water. Tule grass and cattails and milkweed and tall brown rushes grew densely to the water's edge; across the slough, perhaps seventy-five yards wide at that point, thick clumps of anise and sage dotted the flat marshland. In the distance, beyond the Petaluma River itself, the rising black oak-covered foothills of the Sonoma Mountains lay brown and desolate against both summer and winter skies.

You got to Duckblind Slough by way of a narrow dirt road leading off Highway 101 north of Novato, in Marin County. The road wound inland for a mile or so, through aromatic eucalyptus and bay and pepper trees, past a club for trap shooters and the Mira Monte Marina and Boat Launch—a small cluster of buildings which catered to outboard boats and fishermen and water skiers during the summer months. At that point, a sign announced that the road would now pass through private property, and that trespassers would be prosecuted to the fullest extent of the law. Three miles further along, a second private road branched off to the east, crossing a raised bank of railroad spur line tracks; a wooden gate capped with barbed wire and fastened closed with a chain-and-padlock blocked the road there. Duckblind Slough was another half-mile beyond the gate.

The road ended in a small clearing just large enough for four cars if they were parked carefully side by side. Three separate paths led from there to the shacks. The two inland ones were owned by Sonoma County businessmen, who used them sparingly for bass fishing and duck hunting in season, and who seldom if ever used them at any other time. The one on the point belonged to Steve and Andrea Kilduff.

It was almost four when Andrea brought her little Volkswagen into the deserted clearing. She shut off the motor and sat staring at the wind-bent grass and thinking that she was probably crazy for having come all the way up to this desolate spot instead of simply calling her sister, Mona, who lived in suburban comfort in El Cerrito across the Bay. But the idea of having to answer all the questions Mona and her husband, Dave, would ask, and of having to put up with their three pre-school children whom she normally adored but who would undoubtedly send her clawing at the walls in this situation, had not appealed to Andrea at all. She had wanted to be alone—that was a very necessary part of things—and there was no better place for that than Duckblind Slough, where you were almost literally up a depository tributary without due means of locomotion, as a friend of theirs had laughingly suggested when Andrea told him about the shack's location. Besides, Steve would never think of looking for her there; Andrea had never really been one for the spartan life. Oh, she had accompanied him up here a couple of times (anything to get away from the impossible rush of the city), but sitting in a rowboat with a five-horsepower motor and putt-putting in and out of sloughs looking for elusive bass and catfish was not exactly her conception of the ideal vacation. Still, the bleakness, the almost atavistic quality of Duckblind Slough in November, had a certain allure for her now. It was the first place she had thought of—the head shrinkers could make something out of that, all right.

She buttoned her cardigan sweater at her throat and stepped out of the Volkswagen. The wind blowing across the marshlands was gelid, making a low, mournful soul song as it played amongst the tules and cattails, bringing the vague smell of salt and an almost tangible smell of things long dead, as if she had suddenly been thrust backward in time to some primeval era.

Andrea shivered, and then smiled faintly. Next thing you know, she chided herself, you'll be seeing a dinosaur or a tyrannosaur or something come lumbering up to the water to drink, perhaps even to drain the slough dry in its thirst. She shivered again; the thought of all the water being drained from the tributary, of the potential horrors, real or imagined, which lay half-hidden in the sucking mud at its bottom, made a chill twice as cold as the wind's walk along her spine.

Quickly, then, she opened the trunk compartment of the Volkswagen and removed her two pieces of luggage and a cardboard box of food and supplies she had purchased before leaving San Francisco. She left the remainder of her belongings in the car. She carried the suitcases along the vegetation-choked path to the point, set them on the shack's narrow, gap-boarded porch, and returned for the cardboard box, hurrying now. When she had completed the second trip, she fitted the old brass key into the lock and swung the door open.

Two distinct odors greeted her: dry rot and the lingering acridity of fish. Both seemed to flow outward in an unseen wave, as if waiting for escape into the free air, and Andrea recoiled slightly, holding the door open, her nostrils flaring with distaste. After a moment, she carried the suitcases and the box of foodstuffs inside. Shutting the door—her desire for warmth was stronger than her aversion to the shack's smell—she stood surveying the interior. The walls were tar-papered inside as well, and the studs were exposed. In one corner there was an iron potbellied stove which Steve had bought from a junk dealer in San Francisco for fifty dollars three years ago; beside it, stacked neatly against the wall, were a dozen or so circular redwood blocks and some kindling and a pile of yellowed newspapers. A kerosene stove, of the two-burner variety, reposed next to a homemade tin sink in a wood frame. A row of makeshift cabinets hung on the wall above the sink, on both sides of the narrow curtained window there. There was nothing else in the room save for a half-table and two chairs, an ancient wicker chair with a plastic cushion on it, and a folding TV tray sitting off to one side. Through an open doorway leading into the other room—little more than an alcove, really—Andrea could see the wide Army cot that had served as their bed and a scarred, unpainted dresser with three drawers.

Home, she thought ruefully, looking with disrelish at the accumulation of dust and grit which covered the wooden floor. She rubbed her hands together briskly, passing through the doorway into the bedroom alcove. There were two closed doors side by side in the right-hand wall; the nearest, the door to the bathroom (bathroom, now that was really very funny, she thought, a john with a high wooden tank and a long pull-chain, for God's sake, not to mention a cracked enamel sink and an exposed shower that sprayed water almost as muddy as that from the slough, even though the piping was supposed to connect with a county supply line). The other door was padlocked through a hasp: the storage closet.

Andrea unlocked it with another key. From the shelves inside she removed several wool blankets, an old Coleman pressure lantern and a tin of kerosene. She put the blankets on the cot and carried the lantern and kerosene into the other room. Then she found the box of kitchen matches she had bought and took them to the stove and began to build a fire inside, remembering how Steve had done it with bits of kindling from the pile and some of the newspapers. Before long, she had one of the redwood blocks burning; she closed the iron door and stood with her back to the stove, trying to warm herself.

This week alone here was going to be very good for her in a lot of ways, she reflected; she was going to be on her own for a long, long time, having to fend for herself, and there was nothing like disciplining right from the beginning.

When the fire began to crackle hotly inside the pot-belly, Andrea found a broom and a mop in the storage closet and began systematically to clean the interior of the shack.

In the bedroom of her small three-room apartment in Santa Clara, Fran Varner sat moodily sorting her week's laundry and thinking of Larry Drexel.

He could be so strange at times, she thought, putting an orange bath towel into one of the two wicker baskets on the floor at her feet. Like this afternoon, like the way he had yelled at her, practically chased her out of his house, for no reason at all that she could see. She was almost frightened of him at times like that—of course, he'd never hit her or anything, but he had such a violent temper, he'd fly off the handle like a little boy having a tantrum when everything didn't go his way. And he could be so cold and distant, too, as if nothing ever reached him deep inside, as if nothing ever moved him. The only time he was truly warm, truly demonstrative, the only time she really felt spiritually close to him, was when they were making love; when he was inside her, moving, his lips on her breast . . .

Fran's cheeks burned furiously. Oh, you're terrible, she told herself; you're really a wanton, immoral thing. Abruptly, she stood and went to the bedroom window, staring past the frilly curtains at the rear courtyard of the apartment complex. A group of laughing teen-agers, voices raised in shrill merriment, were swimming in the oblong pool beyond the parking area. She watched them for a time, ducking one another in the chill water, making cannonball dives off the low board at one end, oblivious to the cold and the overcast sky, to all but themselves and the very present, the wonderful immediacy of youth.

She had been that way once. A good girl—God, such a meaningless term!—playing good-girl games, thinking good-girl thoughts, pure and innocent, knowing in her heart that when she gave herself to a man it would be on her wedding night . . .

With the carefree incorruption of the young, knowing a foolish lie.

Because she had met Larry Drexel.

And fallen blindly in love with him.

Whatever he was, whatever he felt for her, whatever he said and did to her, she loved him and she would go on loving him.

Fran turned from the window to look toward the near bedroom wall, to where a small calendar hung. There were lines drawn with a red felt pen, through the dates starting with August 28th and running to the present.

Two months and six days.

She was still waiting.

She couldn't put off going to a doctor much longer, she knew that. And if it were true, if the reason she had not had her period in two months and six days was because she was pregnant, it was better to know it for certain—wasn't it?—than to keep falsely hoping she was late because of some hormone imbalance or simple nervousness.

The thing that was bothering her most, of course, the real reason she had put off seeing a doctor for this long, was not the mere fact that she might be pregnant. No, it was having to tell Larry that she had lied about taking the birth control pills, that she had foolishly succumbed to an inbred religious belief that you did not prevent the conception of human life, that she had been going to his bed for the past year on irrational faith alone. It was having to see his face when she told him that, and about the child, having to hear his reply when she asked him not to allow the baby to be born out of wedlock.

She was almost certain what he would say.

He would say that she had done it on purpose, to get him to marry her. And he would refuse.

Fran returned to the bed and sat down again, lighting a cigarette from the pack on the nightstand. No, now no, she couldn't think about such things, she had to put it out of her mind. Maybe she wasn't pregnant after all, maybe everything would be all right given enough time; things always worked out, didn't they?

At five-thirty, the limping man walked to O'Farrell Street and entered a small coffee shop. He sat in an ersatz-leather booth at the rear. A chubby waitress with eyes like slick black buttons took his order: a fried ham sandwich and coffee, no cream.

When the coffee came, the limping man sat watching the steam spiral upward in thin wisps. At the booth across the aisle from him, a young man in a bright blue blazer was talking in low tones to a pretty flame-haired girl. They were holding hands under the table, their knees pressed tightly together. The girl laughed loudly and happily at something the young man said, showing even white teeth and the long slender column of her throat.

Traffic noises filtered in from the street outside in a regular, almost monotonous, rhythm. The limping man lifted his coffee cup, wondering: How am I going to do it this time?

The first one—Blue, in Evanston—had taken the cleverest planning thus far. Blue always went to the Urban Betterment League meeting on Thursday nights, the limping man had discovered; and invariably, he parked his car at the rear of the lot adjacent to the Elks Club, where the meetings were held. The lot was shadowed, unattended during that time, and the limping man had been able to slip quietly and unobtrusively through the parked cars to Blue's new Camaro.

He had waited there for some time, to make sure the lot was completely deserted; then, using a small pipe wrench, he had reached beneath the car and removed the drain plug at the bottom of the gas tank. The resultant flood of gasoline—only six or seven gallons—had been greatly absorbed by the dry, gravelly surface of the lot; the spreading stain was hidden almost completely beneath the Camaro and in the deep shadows. When only a few drops remained in the tank, he had replaced the drain plug. Then, with a Phillips screwdriver, he had extricated the left rear taillight and carefully broken the stop-light bulb with the blade of the screwdriver, to expose the filaments. From his pocket, he had taken a three-foot length of lamp cord, slit on both ends, and, with an alligator clip, attached one side of one end of the cord to the positive portion of the filament in the broken bulb. Using another alligator clip, he had grounded the second side of the cord to the metal taillight frame, first having bent it slightly inward so as to take the clip. The opposite ends of the cord had been stripped bare, and he taped those ends together with electrician's plastic tape, so that the exposed wire tips almost, but not quite, touched—like a spark gap. Then he had removed the gas cap and inserted the cord inside the tank until the wire tips touched bottom, lifted them perhaps a half-inch above it, and then taped the cord in that position with more of the electrician's tape. The entire operation had taken less than ten minutes.

He had been waiting on a side street when Blue and the others came out of the Urban Betterment League meeting. As was usually the case when a man got into his car, simultaneous with starting it, Blue had depressed the brake pedal. The resultant spark from the stop-light filament to the exposed ends of the cord had ignited the fumes in the tank—and the gasoline puddled under the car—and the ensuing explosion had eliminated all traces of the rigging.

The limping man smiled thinly, thinking about the brilliant orange flash which had illuminated the Illinois sky that night, and the booming concussion of the blast. The chubby waitress brought his fried ham sandwich and departed silently. He chewed thoughtfully on the sandwich, his eyes bright and clear as he visualized the violence.

Gray and Red had offered no real challenge. Gray, for example, had been in the habit of working late at his trucking concern three nights each week. The limping man simply waited in the shadows of the garage, having gained entrance through a rear window with a simple spring catch, until Gray made his usual cursory night check of the premises before leaving. Then he had slipped up behind him and wielded a sand-filled stocking. Propping the unconscious Gray against the concrete wall in front of one of the trucks, he had then released the vehicle's hand brake; he had already begun climbing through the rear window again when the loud, satisfying sound of truck and Gray and wall fusing into one reached his ears.

Red had kept his private plane at a small airport on the outskirts of

Philadelphia, in a hangar which a child could have gained access to. The small cold-expander bomb, which had taken the limping man no time at all to construct in his motel room, had fit neatly out of sight beneath one of the wings. When Red had taken the plane up to a certain altitude, when a pre-set atmospheric temperature had been reached, the bomb—and the aircraft—had exploded. There had been, of course, no trace of the small device in the subsequent wreckage.

The limping man finished his sandwich and coffee. Now at hand was the problem of Yellow. How would he do it this time? Perhaps the solution lay with Yellow himself. Yes, there was one particular habit which Yellow had, one that he had noted during the careful surveillance he had made on his previous trip to California. There was little, if any, risk involved if he proceeded along that particular line. Yes. Yes, of course.

Hurriedly, he dabbed at his mouth with a cloth napkin and stepped out of the booth. The man in the blue blazer and the flame-haired girl were still holding hands beneath the table in the booth opposite, eyes smiling warmly at one another.

A slut and her pimp, the limping man thought. He walked quickly to the cash register.

5

The doorbell rang at seven-fifty.

Conscious of a painful tightness in his chest, as if some unknown pressure was slowly constricting his lungs, Steve Kilduff opened the door. The lean, solemn man who stood there said, "Hello, Steve," without expression.

Kilduff nodded wordlessly, and the two men studied each other for a long moment, appraising the effect of the passage of eight years' time. Kilduff thought: He's changed, he's really changed, you can see it in his eyes. He moved aside, swinging the door open wider. Jim Conradin came in past him, walking stiffly, hands held in regimental immobility at his sides. Kilduff closed the door and led the way into the living room, turning when he reached the center to look again at the man who had been his closest friend in the Air Force.

Conradin asked, "Drexel?"

"He's not here yet."

"It's almost eight."

"Yes."

Conradin walked in his stiff way to the sofa and sat down slowly, like an old man seating himself on a park bench. Without looking up, he said, "Have you got a drink, Steve?" and Kilduff realized for the first time that Conradin was drunk. His gaunt-cheeked face was flushed, and there was a vague filminess to his eyes; the effort he was making to appear natural was obvious now, and he was holding himself in check by sheer will.

I am not my brother's keeper, Kilduff thought. He said, "Brandy all right?"

"Fine."

Kilduff took a bottle of Napoleon brandy from the credenza and poured a drink into a small snifter. He carried the glass to Conradin, who accepted it with a steady hand, raising it to his lips, drinking with measured care, his eyes almost closed, trying to bring it off oh-so-casually, and failing, failing badly. Kilduff looked away.

"Well," Conradin said, "some funny thing, isn't it, Steve?"

"What is?"

"The three of us living so close to one another and not knowing it all these years."

"Not so funny," Kilduff said. "You and I are natives of this area, Jim. And Larry was always talking about moving to California."

"Sure, that's right." Conradin drank nervously from his glass. "Listen, what did Drexel tell you? About this meeting tonight?"

"Not much. You?"

"Just that it was important."

"What did he say about the others?"

"They won't be here, that's all."

Kilduff sat down and looked at his hands. "I don't like this, Jim."

"What do you think it means?"

"I don't know."

"It's been more than eleven years."

"Yes," Kilduff said.

"Nobody could have found out after eleven years, could they?" Conradin said. "It has to be something else."

Kilduff said nothing.

Conradin sipped slowly at the brandy. It was very quiet in the shadowed apartment; the only light came from a brass curio lamp next to the couch, bathing one side of Conradin's face in soft white and leaving the other darkly in shadow. After a time he said, "Do you think much about it, Steve? What we did, I mean?"

"Sometimes."

"I can't bury it," Conradin said. "Nothing helps. The guilt keeps eating at me like a cancer. I keep seeing that guard's face—the one I hit. I wake up sweating in the middle of the night, seeing it."

Kilduff did not say anything.

"It bothers you, too, doesn't it?"

"No," Kilduff said.

"Why did we do it, Steve?"

"Why do you suppose? We did it for the money."

"Yes, the money. But I mean, what made us go through with it? It started out as a game, a way to pass the time while we were waiting for our discharge papers, one of those 'let's plot the perfect crime' things that hundreds of people must play every day. What made *us* go through with it?"

"It was foolproof," Kilduff answered. "We realized it would work not only in theory but in actuality, that we could get away with it."

"Do you remember the newspaper accounts?"

"I remember them."

"They said we were incredibly lucky. They said dozens of things could have gone wrong."

"But nothing did, Jim."

"No, nothing did."

"It was a good plan," Kilduff said. The pressure in his chest had increased somewhat, now. "No matter what the papers said."

"We could have been caught so damned easily," Conradin said. "We could have been rotting away in a prison cell all these years."

"Jim," Kilduff said quietly, "Jim, you voted in, just like the rest of us. If there'd been one abstention, we wouldn't have gone through with it, that was the agreement. You knew the risks then; we'd been over them time and again, and you voted in."

"I'll tell you something," Conradin said. He was staring into the brandy snifter. "I was so goddamned scared after I hit that guard that I lost control and shit in my pants. I just sat there in it while we were driving, and I wasn't ashamed."

Jesus, Kilduff thought. He said, "We were all scared."

"I don't think Drexel was. Or Wykopf or Beauchamp."

"Why? Because they did the actual holdup? We drew straws for that, Jim."

"Sure," Conradin said. "Sure, that's right."

The doorbell rang again.

Conradin's hands came together around the brandy snifter, squeezing it convulsively until Kilduff was certain the glass would shatter. He stood abruptly, went into the foyer, and opened the door. Larry Drexel said in his cold voice, "Good to see you again, Steve," and came inside quickly.

After closing the door Kilduff said, "Jim's already here."

"Good," Drexel said. He walked into the living room.

Conradin stood from the couch. "Hello, Larry," he said.

"Jim."

"Can I get you a drink, Larry?" Kilduff asked, thinking: The gracious host, performing all the proper social amenities—this whole thing is incongruous, unreal, like something from a particularly vivid dream. He was breathing through his mouth now, in short, silently asthmatic inhalations.

Drexel shook his head, moving toward the sofa, sitting on the opposite end from Conradin. He wore an expensive sports outfit—a hound's-tooth jacket and knife-crease charcoal slacks and a tailored white shirt open at the throat; his Bally shoes glistened with black polish. Conradin and Kilduff—respectively dressed in a sheepskin jacket and a pair of blue denims, and an old alpaca golf sweater over a rumpled pair of tan trousers—looked shabby and subservient in comparison. Kilduff remembered that Drexel had always demonstrated the need to dominate, to be the focal point; he hadn't changed at all.

Drexel's eyes shifted to Kilduff. "The old school reunion," he said with no trace of levity.

"Except that half of the class is missing," Kilduff said in the same humorless tone. "What's this all about?"

Conradin's hands were still wrapped tightly around the brandy snifter. "Yes, let's have it, Larry."

"All right," Drexel said. "Here it is, pure and simple; last month, in October, Cavalacci and Wykopf and Beauchamp were killed, all of them, in separate accidents. Cavalacci, when his car mysteriously blew up in a parking lot; Wykopf, in front of a truck that unaccountably slipped its hand brake in a garage he owned; Beauchamp, when his private plane suddenly exploded in midair."

"Sweet Jesus," Conradin said reverently. He drained the remaining brandy in the snifter.

Kilduff felt an odd coldness on the back of his neck, but that was all, really. Cavalacci and Wykopf and Beauchamp were men he had known eleven years ago, half-faceless men viewed with objective recollection, and he did not experience any real sense of loss at the news of their deaths. He said, "How do you know all this?"

Drexel's lips pursed into a thin white line. "If it matters, I've kept tabs on all of you over the years. I'm careful, damned careful, and I never did approve of the idea of absolute separation. I knew where you all had come from originally, and I figured that you'd either return to your home towns or stay in Illinois after the Statute ran out. I checked telephone directories and city directories and made a few discreet inquiries here and there and took subscriptions to local newspapers; after a while I found out where each of you were and what you were doing."

"I don't like the idea of that," Kilduff said. "The agreement—"

"To hell with the agreement," Drexel said coldly. "You'd better be thankful I did it that way. It might save your life."

"What does that mean?"

"For Christ's sake, do you think it's *coincidence* that three of us died in the same month, all in unexplained accidents?"

Kilduff moistened his lips. "What else could it be?"

"Murder," Drexel said. "That's what else it could be."

The single word—*murder*—seemed to hang suspended in the now-silent room, an embodied entity that held Conradin and Kilduff transfixed for a long moment. Finally Kilduff said very softly, "You're crazy, Larry."

"Am I?"

"You actually believe the three of them were murdered?"

"I'm damned if I can accept the coincidence of all three dying in the same month. Two of them, maybe; but not all three."

"Is that why you called this meeting?"

"Yes."

"Because you think the three of *us* are next? Because of Granite City?"

"Yes, that's just what I think."

Conradin stood and walked jerkily to the credenza. "Larry, there's nobody who'd do a thing like you're suggesting. A man would have to be insane . . ."

"That's right," Drexel said. "A man who *is* insane, a man who somehow found out we were the ones who robbed that armored car in Granite City, a man who's decided in his twisted mind that we're directly responsible for a lot of things that happened to *him* as a result of the holdup. A man like Leo Helgerman."

"Who?" Kilduff asked.

"Helgerman, the goddamned Mannerling guard Jim hit when he blew his cool in that parking lot."

"Oh Christ!" Conradin said. He poured his snifter full again and drank it off. He had begun to tremble noticeably. His face blanched.

Kilduff said, "Larry, you're dreaming!"

"The hell I am," Drexel said vehemently. "He was partially paralyzed with spinal damage for a while, wasn't he? It was in the papers how bitter he was, how badly he wanted all of us caught."

"That's a natural reaction, after what happened."

"Maybe it turned into an *un*natural vendetta."

Kilduff stared at him incredulously. "Are you saying Helgerman's mind snapped and he's become some kind of avenging angel who's killing us off one by one eleven years later? Larry, you can't expect us to accept an incredible fantasy like that."

"Goddamn it, stranger things have happened."

"So have stranger *coincidences* than three of us dying by accident in the same month."

"Look, do you think I *like* the idea? It scares the hell out of me. But there's the possibility that I'm right, and you'd better face up to it."

Conradin came back to the couch with the snifter full again. He sat down and stared at the dark liquid as if it held some kind of hypnotic fascination for him. But Kilduff felt a subtle release of tension; all the melodrama on the phone and all the cold, frightened sweating of the afternoon and early evening had been unnecessary. The pressure in his chest had begun to abate. He said, "How could Helgerman have found out we were the ones? It's been eleven years, Larry, *eleven years.* The entire state of Illinois hasn't been able to find out in that time."

"I don't have any answers," Drexel said. "I'm not psychic. I'm just telling you the way it is."

"Well, all right. Suppose you're right. Just suppose you are. What do you think we ought to do?"

"I'm not sure."

"We can't go to the police," Kilduff said. "That's obvious. And I'm not going to run on the strength of a monstrous improbability. I wouldn't know how to run anyway."

"You think we ought to just sit around and wait, is that it?" Drexel asked. "Until another one of us dies in an 'accident'?"

"What the hell else *is* there for us to do?" Kilduff said. "We haven't got any concrete reason to panic, no proof that the others died except by accident, no proof that Helgerman is insane and a murderer, or, for Christ's sake, that he's even still *alive.*"

"Then we've got to find out," Drexel said. "One way or another."

"How?" Kilduff asked. "Larry, we're three guys pushing thirty-five who somehow managed to pull off a major crime when we were little more than kids. We're no more experienced now than we were then;

if anything, we're less equipped today—we haven't got that crazy, irrational, what-the-screw disregard for what happens tomorrow or next week or next month. Do you expect us to carry a .45 automatic in a shoulder holster like some Spillane character, peering furtively into shadows and asking veiled questions in dingy bars?"

Drexel put his hands flat on his knees, his cold eyes darkly flashing. "That's a nice speech, Steve," he said tonelessly.

"Listen," Kilduff said, "all I'm trying to say is that I can't accept the idea that Helgerman is going around picking us off one by one because we robbed an armored car eleven years ago and he ended up on disability. If you believe it, then you can do what you want."

"But you're not going to do anything."

"No," Kilduff said. "I'm not."

Without looking at him, Drexel said to Conradin, "And what about you, Jim? Is that your position, too?"

"I don't know," Conradin answered slowly. "I don't know what my position is."

"All right, then," Drexel said. Abruptly, he got on his feet. "You're both damned fools, curled up in your secure, complacent little worlds like a couple of foetuses and you think you're inviolate, you think nothing out of the past can reach you any more. Well, all right. I don't much care what happens to either one of *you,* but I care about my own neck and I'm going to do something." He took two small white business cards from the inside pocket of his jacket and threw them on the coffee table. "If you decide to face reality, you can reach me at either of the numbers on those cards."

Without waiting for either of the others to say anything, he crossed to the door and went out, slamming it shut behind him.

Kilduff and Conradin sat in unbroken silence for several moments, a pair of sculpted figures in some impressionistic museum exhibit. At length, Kilduff said quietly, "It's impossible. You know that, too, don't you, Jim? The whole idea of it is inconceivable."

Conradin gave a slow, tremulous sigh. "Is it?" he asked. "Is it really, Steve? Or are we too afraid to admit the chance of it to ourselves, like Drexel said? Are we too afraid that we wouldn't be able to cope with it if it were somehow true?"

"No," Kilduff said emphatically.

Conradin picked up one of the white cards from the coffee table and put it into the pocket of his sheepskin jacket. "I'd better be going now."

"What are you planning to do?"

"Nothing," Conradin answered. He started toward the door, and Kilduff stood and followed him there. "Except maybe say a prayer that Drexel is wrong and you're right."

"I'm right," Kilduff said.

"I hope to God you are."

"We don't have anything to worry about."

"Don't we?" Conradin asked, opening the door.

"No, nothing."

"Except maybe ourselves," Conradin said. "Good night, Steve." And he was gone.

Except maybe ourselves.

Kilduff shut the door and returned to the living room and sat in the chair again, he seemed to be doing a lot of sitting in that chair. He sat there and stared at nothing and thought about Drexel and what he had said, and Conradin and what he had said, and about Cavalacci and Wykopf and Beauchamp lying in cold dark boxes beneath the cold dark earth; he thought about them for a long, long time . . .

. . . *And Andrea came to him in the darkness of the tiny cottage bedroom, nude and unashamed, an alabaster naiad haloed in sweet innocence, diminutive and Elysian and proud in the so very pale honeymoon-shine drifting in through the minute apertures in the bamboo blinds. She came to him with her arms held wide and her mouth scrubbed free of rouge, her eyes lidded with unaffected, loving sensuality, her breasts small-white and tense, the nipples and aureoles fine exquisite black diamonds, the melanoid triangle of her pubic hair a swath of the softest velvet demurely hiding the pure still waters beneath. She came to him with his name on her lips and lay beside him on the conjugal bed, breathing warm honey against his neck, warm honey; and there was the taste of her, feel of her, an aching of acute pleasure in his genitals. He was moving within her now—strange, there seemed to have been no virginal obstruction, no innocence, strange. And then he was saying her name over and over, "Andrea! Andrea! Andrea!" moving faster and faster and faster but she began to dissolve beside him, no no no, began to fade into a nebulous shadow, no no, and then she was gone, no, gone, and he was alone again, alone not in the tiny cottage bedroom with its honeymoon-shine but alone in a dank, fetid cave, so very dark, and the smell of millenniums of de-*

cay was in his nostrils. He shrank into a corner and felt the viscid slime of subterranean stone against his nude body, and then from across that malefic cavern there came a movement, a slithering of something unimaginable, a foul sucking, crawling sound, and he shrank deeper into the corner, terrified, seeing a fulvous pinpoint of light appear before him, gradually expanding, illuminating a shape within the hazy glow, a shape which became a faceless, monstrous thing of such unspeakable horror that he opened his mouth and began to scream with his very soul, for the nameless faceless thing was coming nearer, coming closer, reaching for him with an extremity that dripped putrefaction . . .

Kilduff came up out of the chair in a single convulsive leap, standing with his heart plunging impossibly in his chest and the length of his body encased in a thick mucilaginous sweat. At first he was still in that cave, still cowering just beyond the reach of the horror in his dream; but then his mind began to clear and the trembling of his body ceased and he realized it had been only that: a dream. His eyes moved upward to the sunburst clock on the wall: twelve-fifteen. He had mesmerized himself, sitting in the chair, into the nether world of the subconscious.

He went into the kitchen and drank a glass of ice water from the refrigerator; his throat was raw and parched. In the bedroom he undressed and slid between the clean, cool sheets of the bed and closed his eyes. And when fatigue brought sleep flooding over him finally—

Andrea came to him in the darkness of the tiny cottage bedroom . . .

6

The limping man left the Graceling Hotel at eleven o'clock Sunday morning. He walked through heavy damp fog—one hand firmly grasping the handle of the American Tourister briefcase, and suspended over his right shoulder by a thin carrying strap, a cracked vinyl case containing an inexpensive pair of Japanese-manufactured binoculars—to the parking garage on Geary, where he had left the rented Mustang the previous afternoon.

He presented his claim check to the attendant on duty, and when the car was brought down from one of the upper floors, he locked the briefcase and the binoculars inside the trunk. Moments later, he drove up to the street.

It was still early, of course, he knew that—there really was nothing he could do until after dark—but leaving now assured him of plenty of time to select a place of concealment from which he could observe Yellow's movements. Besides, Yellow's moment was close at hand now—very close, perhaps as close as that very night—and the limping man was possessed with a certain nervous excitement, the same excitement he had experienced prior to Red and Gray and Blue. He could not simply remain in his hotel room for the entire day.

With his right hand he manipulated the dials on the automobile radio until he found a station which played old standards. He turned up the volume, thinking of Yellow as he drove with cautious rapidity through the chill, mist-shrouded San Francisco morning.

In the shack in Duckblind Slough, Andrea Kilduff sat bundled in her wool jacket at the wooden half-table, drinking a cup of hot black coffee. She had not slept well at all—had lain shivering beneath the heavy blankets on the Army cot, listening to that damned wind howl across the morass and across the expanse of the slough like the collective wail of souls in purgatory—and she felt chilled and cross and very much alone on this Sunday morning.

She had cleaned the shack from top to bottom the previous day, going over everything with mop and broom and dustcloth and soapy water at least twice, putting herself into the chore with an almost mechanized fervency, making it last until day had receded into night. As a result, the two-room interior was spotlessly fastidious—almost, she thought, surveying now her labor in the light of morning, comfortably livable. Almost.

Andrea finished her coffee and carried the cup to the tin sink and washed it out carefully, turning it upside down on the wood drainboard. She looked briefly out of the window above the sink, at the wind-swept grasses covering the inland area within her vision, at the leaden sky with its promise soon of rain, and then she turned away and sat down again at the table. She lifted the ostentatiously dust-jacketed novel she had brought with her (four hundred pages, very erotic—makes you ever so terribly horny, dear, a friend of hers had told her), but she put it down almost immediately. She didn't feel like reading—not that she felt like sitting either, because she didn't. Well, she was a fine one; she'd been out on her own for less than one day and already her own company bored her to tears. But there was nothing to *do*, nothing to keep her mind occupied the way the house-cleaning had done yesterday; at home, she had been able to call one of her friends on the telephone or go out shopping or driving or visiting if she became bored; but here, there was just nothing to do . . .

Well, I'm certainly not *chained* here, am I? she asked herself. I can leave, can't I? Well, of course I can; I'm *not* a prisoner in this shack, after all. There's nothing that says I can't leave for the day any time I want to.

The thoughts became a firm resolution in her mind, and she stood and reached for her purse. Yes, a drive was just the thing, into San Rafael, she decided; there was one large shopping center which remained open on Sundays. She could browse leisurely there, have lunch, perhaps even go to a movie tonight. That was certainly better than just sitting here in this now-comfortable, now-livable little shack in the middle of nowhere that she knew she was a darned fool for coming to in the first place, in spite of all her nice rationalizations.

Buttoning the wool jacket to her throat, Andrea went to the door and stepped outside.

To escape momentarily from all the hundreds of little things that had begun to remind her of Steve from the moment she first set foot inside the shack, from all the memories that a thousand cleanings could never remove from its omniscient walls.

Standing at the edge of a small, grassy slope in Golden Gate Park, his hands pressed deep into the pockets of his topcoat, Steve Kilduff looked out over the flat, shallow water of Lloyd Lake. What I've got to do, he told himself, is be practical; I've got to put yesterday out of my mind, blank it out—Andrea and Drexel and Granite City—blank it all out with cold clear calculation and think about what *I'm* going to do now, now that the money's almost gone and I'm about to be faced with the prospect of starvation. So it looks like a job, eight-to-five or equivalent, because I sure as hell don't qualify for welfare; digging ditches or pumping gas or clerking in an office, brown-nosing the boss's ass for that Christmas bonus and that ten-dollar semi-annual raise—why not? The trouble before was I wanted too much, expected too much; once you've got money, you acquire a taste for luxury, for *money*, and you can't reconcile yourself to menial labor for menial wages. That was the trouble, all right, that was exactly what the trouble was, so the thing to do is go down to one of the employment agencies tomorrow and tell them I'll take anything so long as it's honest, tell them . . . well, now, that was pretty funny, wasn't it? *Take anything so long as it's honest.* Oh, Lord, that was really pretty damned funny, old Public Enemy Number One, The Man Who Helped Pull Off One Of The Few Really Big Unsolved Crimes In The Country, why, yes sir, I'll take anything you have open just so long as it's honest . . .

El Peyote was a combination cocktail lounge and Mexican restaurant on South First Street in San Jose—a low, stucco, Spanish-architected building with a center patio replete with fountain and heavy tables and strolling *mariachis* for outdoor summer dining. It catered to a varied clientele, from the surrounding suburban elite to the *pachuco* of San Jose's large Mexican population. Five men had been knifed—two of them, fatally—in El Peyote's dark interior lounge in the six years since Larry Drexel had opened it, and instead of harming business, it brought out the crowds.

As far as Drexel was concerned, if people wanted to pay for the prospect of seeing some spic with his belly ripped away, holding in his entrails with one bloody hand, then that was all right with him. He had raised his prices ten percent after the last incident, three months previously; with a winking smile, he had told Juano—his three-hundred-pound headwaiter-cum-bouncer—that the increase was a kind of entertainment tax, what the hell.

At five o'clock Sunday afternoon, Drexel was sitting in his darkly furnished office upstairs above the lounge, drinking *aquardiente*, and staring broodingly at a large reproduction in oil of a portion of a mural by Diego Rivera, which covered the wall immediately behind his desk. He felt edgy and restless, had felt that way ever since learning of Beauchamp's death, and spending the better part of the day in his office hadn't helped matters any. And then there was the meeting last night—that had been a mistake right down the line. Conradin and Kilduff were a pair of spineless bastards and he should have known better than to expect anything from them, not after so many years had elapsed. Well, if they wanted to sit around and pretend that their goddamn lives weren't in danger, then that was rum-dandy; but he was damned if *he* would do the same thing. The both of them could go screw off. He'd take care of Number One and only Number One from now on.

Driving back to Los Gatos from Kilduff's apartment last night, he had decided on a direct course of action—and that meant locating Leo Helgerman, which in turn meant returning to Illinois for the first time since 1962. He had debated leaving immediately—today, Sunday—but there was the fact of a certain contract meeting in Wade Cosgreave's law offices Monday morning at ten sharp. Drexel had spent three months negotiating with a stubborn old fart named Esteban Martinez for purchase of Cantina del Flores, a restaurant-and-lounge combine in Campbell, similar to El Peyote, and Cosgreave had all but clinched the deal just last week; there remained only the formalities of signing the contract and working out financial arrangements with banking representatives. But there were other interested parties besides himself, and he knew that if he canceled the meeting tomorrow, he would run the risk of ruffling Martinez's feathers enough to make him sell to one of the other bidders—and Cantina del Flores was too juicy a plum (the first such plum in a carefully mapped plan for expansion), to risk losing out on.

Drexel had called the airlines reservations desk at San Francisco International that morning, reserving passage on the three-thirty flight for Chicago on Monday afternoon. One more day wouldn't make any difference, not so long as he was watchful and—

A knock sounded on the door, soft, almost hesitant. Drexel swiveled reflexively toward the door, his hands gripping the lacquered edge of his desk just above the center drawer, his body tensing. "Who is it?" he called out sharply.

"It's Fran, Larry," a quiet, familiar voice said from the other side of the door.

Drexel relaxed. Damn, but he was edgy. He was beginning to jump at shadows again, the way he had done those three years in Illinois, waiting. Ease down, he told himself, cool now. Then he stood and went over and unlocked the door.

Fran Varner came in past him, wearing her hostess outfit—a short, flaming scarlet *enredo* and a sleeveless, low-cut, very tight white blouse. Her smile was hesitant, like the knock had been. She said, "Hi," turning to face him.

"Hi, kid," Drexel said.

"I was wondering if . . . you were going to take me home."

"Didn't you bring your car?"

"Well, yes, but—"

Drexel grinned. Yeah, he had to ease down all right, and there was one sure way of doing that. He let his eyes walk appreciatively along her smooth, tawny legs and upward across her flat stomach to the swell of her breasts. "Sure," he said. "I know."

She lowered her eyes. "You're not still mad at me, are you?"

"Mad at you?"

"You hardly said two words to me today, and after yesterday . . . well, I thought—"

Drexel put his hands on her shoulders. "Don't be silly, kid," he said softly. "I've had some things on my mind, that's all."

"It wasn't me?"

"No, it wasn't you."

"Larry . . ."

He brought her up close against him, kissing her, letting his tongue flick over her lips. Her arms went around his neck as she returned his kiss passionately, tongue meeting his, her body fitting to his. He took his left hand from her shoulder and let it slide down to cup one of her breasts, kneading gently; breath came in sharp, staccato explosions from her nostrils. But when his hand left her breast and moved down to her thigh, coming up under the wrap-around skirt, she broke the kiss and stepped back, face flushed, chest lifting and falling rapidly. She said in a whisper, "I'll make supper for you tonight, if you want."

"Sure," he said.

"Fried chicken and cole slaw and apple turnovers."

"That's the ticket."

"I love you, Larry."

"Sure, baby," he said. "Listen, you go down to the lounge and wait for me. I'll be along in a couple of minutes."

"All right," Fran said. "Don't be long."

"A couple of minutes."

He watched the movement of her hips under the skirt as she left the office, thinking: Some sweet piece of ass, all right, he would be calm as a baby after a session in the sack with her. When the door had closed behind her, he returned to his desk and slid the center drawer open. He lifted out the .38-caliber Smith and Wesson revolver that he had bought and registered and received a permit for just after opening El Peyote. He put the gun in his left-hand jacket pocket and took his overcoat from the rack near the door; the weight of the revolver, which pulled down the left side of the suit jacket, was not noticeable when he had the overcoat buttoned.

He wasn't going unprepared, that was for sure. Helgerman would find one hell of a hot reception waiting for him if he came after Larry Drexel before Drexel had the chance to look *him* up . . .

7

When Jim Conradin had been a senior in high school, he had read as part of an advanced English Literature course Joseph Conrad's *The Heart of Darkness.* Toward the end of that richly symbolic novella, a German exploiter named Kurtz lies dying in the pilot room of a steamer in the atavistic jungles of the Congo. Maddened, but still capable of moments of rational lucidity, Kurtz cries out to the narrator of the story, Marlow, with perhaps his final breath: "The horror! The horror!"

Which meant what? Conradin's instructor had asked in an essay assignment. The horror of death? Of the primordial wilderness and what it can do to a man? Or of something else, as suggested by the events of the story? Conradin had written that "the horror," Kurtz's and every man's, was the sight of his own soul, stripped bare before his eyes to reveal it for what it could and had become. The "heart of darkness," then, he had said, was not the Congo of the late eighteen hundreds—but the very essence of man.

As he paced cat-nervous from one room to another in the big white house on the northern flat of Bodega Bay, Conradin was oddly reminded of that story, and of his perception at age eighteen. He took short, quick sips from a tumbler half filled with sour mash bourbon as he paced—sitting room, kitchen, upstairs hall, cellar workshop, bedroom, storage porch—stopping for a moment to stare out at the black wall of fog enshrouding the house, moving once more, thinking: *The horror! The horror!*

He was in the sitting room again when Trina came in from the hallway, her face mirroring concern, confusion—the same fright which had seized her the day before. She was kneading a floral-bordered dish towel between her hands as if it were biscuit dough. "Supper's ready, Jim," she said quietly.

"I'm not hungry, Trin."

"You haven't eaten anything all day. It's after seven."

"I'm just not hungry."

She walked up close to him and stood staring into his eyes, trying to read them, and failing. She said, "Jim, what is it? What's troubling you? What happened last night?"

"Nothing happened last night."

"Please, dear. You've been acting so . . . strangely since you came home from San Francisco."

"I'm all right," he said. "You go ahead and eat now."

"Not without you."

"Do I have to be there for you to eat?"

"No, of course not, but—"

"Well, then?" Conradin finished the dark liquid in the tumbler and moved to the tray of liquor set on an oval table near one wall. He lifted a black-labeled bottle. The bottle, unopened that morning, was now less than a quarter full.

Behind him, Trina said, "I wish you wouldn't drink any more."

"Trin, please go eat your supper." He filled the tumbler, replaced the bottle on the tray, and turned. "Can't you see I want to be left alone?"

"Yes, I can see that," she said. "But *why*? Why are you shutting me out this way?"

"I'm not shutting you out."

"Yes you are. You won't tell me anything about this mysterious San Francisco trip, you won't talk to me at all. The only things you've done today are drink and pace like some caged animal. I'm frightened, Jim. I really am. I'm frightened because I can't understand what's happening to you."

Conradin moistened his lips. "Honey, there's nothing to understand. Nothing's happening to me. I'm just feeling out of sorts today, that's all. You know how I hate the winter."

"You didn't used to hate anything."

"People change," Conradin said. "People . . . change."

"Yes, they change. They change and they become strangers. You're a stranger to me now."

"Trin . . ."

"I'm your wife," she said. "Don't you think I *know* when something's wrong? Tell me what it is, Jim. Confide in me—you can do that, can't you?"

"No. No, I can't do that."

"Why can't you?"

"I just can't."

Abruptly, tears began to form in Trina's eyes. "I . . ." she began, but then the tears came in a rush and she fled the room. Conradin stood there, looking into the hallway after her. He drank the contents of the tumbler in a single convulsive swallow, put the glass down carefully on the eagle's-claw stand in the hallway, and crossed to the winding staircase which led to the second floor. In his and Trina's bedroom, he took his sheepskin jacket from the closet and put it on and scraped his car keys off the dresser. He descended the stairs again.

Trina was waiting for him, her eyes tinged in red, but she had dried the tears in the downstairs bathroom and was standing very straight and rigid. She said, "Where are you going, Jim?"

"For a drive."

"To where?"

"I don't know," Conradin said. "Just for a drive."

"Jim, please don't go out tonight."

"Why not?"

"The fog is so heavy . . ."

"The fog is always heavy in the winter."

"Please don't go."

"I'll be back in an hour or two."

"You won't have any more to drink, will you? Promise me you won't have any more to drink."

"All right, I won't have any more to drink."

"Jim, I . . ."

Conradin stepped forward and brushed his lips across her forehead; then, quickly, he walked to the front door, opened it, and started out.

"Be careful!" Trina called urgently behind him.

"Yes," he said. He shut the door, bowing his head against the drizzle-like chilliness of the fog, his footfalls making soft, brittle sounds on the crushed-shell surface of the drive. He reached the car parked facing out and slid inside and brought the engine to life. He switched on the headlights—a pair of saffron eyes in the vaporous darkness—and then took the car down the inclined drive and onto Shoreline Highway, turning east there toward Highway 1.

When he reached Highway 1, he swung north, driving rapidly and with full concentration. He followed the winding, two-lane highway for several miles. The night seemed almost completely deserted; once, when headlights flickered briefly in the Dodge's rear-view mirror, Conradin tensed and his hands gripped the wheel more tightly; but after a short time, the shine of them retreated and then disappeared completely.

A few minutes later, Conradin came in sight of a thin strip of state road, attached to a wide circle of macadam, which wound off to the west. The right forward curve of the circle touched the highway and was designed for cars coming in from the south, or coming out to the north; the left forward curve did likewise, designed for cars coming in from the north, or coming out to the south. In the middle of the circle, imbedded in gravel and cement, was a large redwood sign with gold letters that were almost obliterated by the fog. It read: GOAT ROCK.

Conradin nodded to himself, slowing, putting on his directional signal. He turned into the right curve of the circle and entered the state road. Walled by shale bluffs on the right and steep cut-away cliffs heavily overgrown with anise and thistle and sage and wild strawberry on the left, the road dog-legged and twisted its way seaward; Conradin knew it well, had traversed it hundreds, if not thousands, of times, and he had no trouble negotiating its precarious width, even with the roiling mist shredding in his head lamps like fine gossamer cobwebs.

Exactly one mile from the highway, there was a graveled turn-out area and another redwood and gold-lettered sign; this one read: BLIND BEACH. Conradin brought the Dodge in there, nosing up to one of the black asphalt bumpers at its far edge. He sat there for a moment before darkening the car, and then stepped out into the frigid night.

A numbing sea wind blew in across the turn-out, and Conradin felt it billow his clothing and slap wet fingers across his face. He walked to the seaward edge and stood looking out. On his left, now only a vague outline, a shadow slightly grayer than the fog, was a high flat rock covered with nests and lichen and bird droppings—the home of thousands of seagulls and cormorants; and on his right, perhaps a mile away by the state road, was the huge eroded visage of Goat Rock, with a gaping half-moon cut in its back by man in search of raw materials, and beyond it the village of Jenner, where Russian River empties into the Pacific Ocean. But none of these were discernible from where Conradin stood, not on this night.

He let his eyes drop to the inclined dirt side of the short slope below him. Even though he could not see it, he knew the exact location of the narrow, meandering pebble-and-sand path that led down the face of the cliff to Blind Beach. The beach itself—a circumscribed strip of clean white sand, extending for perhaps a quarter mile—was so named because even on the clearest of summer days, it was hidden from view by the convex proportions of the cliff side.

The path began at the far end of the turn-out, near where Conradin had parked his car and near the twin gray outhouses which served as public rest rooms; but instead of taking that lengthy, if somewhat safer, route, Conradin made his way carefully down the short dirt slope. He intercepted the path some one hundred feet below the turn-out, in a narrow ledge-like area. He paused there, looking down at the growth of sage and tule grass and bleak, clustered stalks that would be wild dandelions and purple lupins in the spring—all clinging to the side of the precipice: amorphous green-black shadows in the fog.

Slowly, carefully, Conradin began to make his way down the arduous path to the beach. When he reached it, some time later, in a driftwood-choked crescent sheltered by the cliff walls, he turned diagonally to the south and the black line of the sea.

He walked the length of Blind Beach for over an hour, listening to the sonorous lament of the winter wind and the crash of the angry foaming black waves hurtling again and again and again upon the passive white sand, like an ardent lover with a frigid mate, evoking no response except that of infinite tolerance, growing more angry with each thrust, and more frustrated and more determined, all for nothing except to come, and to rest, and to begin again—futilely, eternally.

"I wish I knew what to do," he said aloud, and the wind swirled loose sand against his body and swirled the words away almost as soon as they left his lips. "I wish to God above I knew what to do."

But he didn't know; he knew only that he couldn't go on this way, being slowly torn apart from within, the guilt growing more unbearable with each passing day, seeing Helgerman's face just as clearly now as on that day eleven years ago; and now this new fear: Helgerman not only as a ghost but as a real and imminent danger, Helgerman as an insane purveyor of vengeance born of a senseless act he, Conradin, had committed out of fear, Helgerman smiting him down as he had smote Helgerman, an eye for an eye, a blow for a blow . . .

Yes, and Kurtz and what he saw when he looked at his own soul and what Jim Conradin was beginning to see in the examination of *his* soul.

The alternatives were clear, of course.

He could, somehow, through some means, find peace with himself.

He could very easily end up suffering a complete mental breakdown.

He could commit suicide.

The latter alternative was not a new one to him. The idea of taking his own life had first occurred to him two years ago, during a particularly bad winter—constant rain, too much time for the thinking. But he had rejected it, exactly as he had rejected it this afternoon. It was not that he lacked the courage, that his fear of death was inordinately strong—no, it was because of Trina, of what such an act would do to her; he could not sacrifice her happiness and her well-being for his own jaded salvation. Still, with the pressure building now, building almost intolerably, all hope of ever finding an inner peace gone now, death or madness were the only ultimates which he could look forward to—and death was by far the more preferable of the two.

Long walks along the beach here, where he could smell and taste and feel the sea near him, usually served to calm him; but on this night Conradin felt even more strung out than he had before leaving the house in Bodega Bay. The cold had begun to reach him too, sending prickles of ice moving, slithering, across his shoulders, and he shivered and began to walk rapidly through the damp sand toward the pebbled path. A mug of coffee, laced with a little mash, and the warmth of wool blankets and soft sheets and Trina lying close to him—perhaps he would make love to her tonight, perhaps he would find some degree of quietude after that; he might be satiated, relieved momentarily of some of the tensions, yes, yes.

He reached the path and began the ascent, eyes cast on the surface barely discernible beneath his canvas shoes. He climbed steadily, surely, feeling the wind tug at his body, clinging to rocks and craggy overhangs, breathing deeply through his mouth. Finally he reached the ledge-like area at the foot of the dirt slope; he paused there, his back to the path's edge and to the gray nothingness, drawing air into his labored lungs, not looking up.

And then out of the ashen swirling vapor comes a stealthy shadowed movement and a face appears as if by some strange necromancy, disembodied, floating, a terrible white face Jim Conradin recognizes almost instantly, but before he can think or speak or act, a hand appears below the face and thrusts itself against his chest, thrusts with such tremendous force that Conradin, who is standing flat-footed and unprepared, flies backward to the rim of the precipice and his canvas shoes slip on the moist vegetation and suddenly he is touching air, touching emptiness, falling, falling, turning in a graceless somersault like a puppet with its strings cut, mouth opening to emit a short piercing scream that lasts for only a second or two, ending abruptly as first his torso and then his head strike a jagged outcropping of rock, splitting his head open like kindling under a woodsman's axe, killing him instantly, and his body plummets off the convexity of the cliff side into space and falls free, slow motion through the sea of fog, to bury itself half-deep in the cold damp sand of the beach one thousand feet below . . .

Green Tuesday and Wednesday

8

On Tuesday, the rains came down.

The storm which had been threatening the Bay Area since Saturday broke with vehemence at six o'clock of that morning, and by noon San Francisco and its surrounding counties lay sodden beneath the steady deluge of cold, dark, hard rain. The skies were limned with black threads on a dove-colored background—and the fog had evaporated, as if the downpour had magically triggered some huge and invisible suction machine. The sea wind blew the pungent smells of brine and wet pavement and damp leaves and gray loneliness. Winter, having arrived at last, had come with all its chattels; it would be staying on.

In the small town of Sebastopol, some fifteen miles inland and to the southeast of Bodega Bay, rain, like semi-translucent sheets of heavy plastic, slanted down on a low, modern redwood-and-brick building a few blocks from South Main Street. But the wide rectangular redwood sign on the fronting lawn was easily discernible through the downpour; it read: SPENCER AND SPENCER MEMORIAL CHAPEL.

Inside the mortuary, in a huge and high-ceilinged parlor, an unseen organist played soft dirge music and there was the almost cloying fragrance of chrysanthemum and gardenia. Ringed by variegated sprays and floral horseshoes, an unadorned casket rested on a bier of ferns and white carnations at the upper half of the parlor. The coffin's lid had been closed and sealed.

To the immediate right, on a dais in a tiny alcove, Trina Conradin sat with her hands clasped tightly at her breast, her head bowed. Her dead husband's mother wept softly, convulsively, agonizingly, on one of the brown folding chairs beside her; her own mother held Mrs. Conradin's hand and whispered gentle, useless words in a tremulous voice. Trina's eyes were dry, like those of her father and Jim's father, both of whom sat stoically, like Oriental stone carvings, on her other side. She had done her crying in the cold darkness of Sunday night, when Jim hadn't come home from his drive and the terrible premonition, the fear which had been rising within her, manifested itself and she had reported him missing; and throughout the somber opalescence of yesterday—after a Sonoma County Sheriff's Deputy had found him lying broken at the foot of the cliff at Blind Beach. She was purged now, empty, barren.

Trina lifted her head slowly, with an inaudible exhalation of breath, and looked upon the some two dozen folding chairs which had been set into neat, symmetrical rows on the deep-pile maroon carpet of the parlor. They were perhaps only a third occupied now, and the services were due to begin any moment.

Her eyes went from each man and woman who had thought enough of Jim Conradin—the man good and kind and gentle—to attend his funeral, to pay their last respects. Troy Gardner, who had been Jim's best man at their wedding, and his wife; the owner of the processing plant where Jim sold most of his catches; their neighbors on Bodega Flat; the old man who had once been a sailing master and who was somewhat of an institution around the area; and—

Trina studied the faces of the final two mourners, sitting at the rear of the parlor side by side. A tall, muscular man with thick black hair and hollow cheeks, wearing a charcoal suit and a starched white shirt and a muted tie; and a dark Latin man, who reminded her vaguely of some actor, dressed similarly but more expensively. She couldn't recall ever having seen either of them before. Strangers? No, certainly not. They must have known Jim at one time or another, perhaps in the Air Force . . .

The service was mercifully brief.

Eventually the mourners rose from their chairs and formed a single line at the far side of the parlor and began to file one by one past the closed coffin and past the family alcove, their hands clasped at their waists, avoiding the eyes of the family in deference to their grief. Finally they entered the vestibule for the momentary assemblage of the funeral cortege, which would take them first to the tiny hamlet of Bodega—inland and south of Bodega Bay—to a small white church on a hill there, and then to the old cemetery on Fallon Road, not far from the sea.

The two men whom Trina did not know drew by the coffin—the final links in the too-short chain of mourners—and the dark Latin man walked beyond the alcove rapidly, with his head held erect and his hands swinging free at his sides. The tall man lagged several steps behind him, and when he came parallel to the family he paused, hesitant, uncertain, and then raised his head, and his eyes touched Trina's for a brief second. She saw in them compassion and sadness and—something else, an indefinable something which made them seem haunted.

He opened his mouth, closed it, opened it again, and then said, "Mrs. Conradin . . . I'm sorry, Mrs. Conradin." She was so surprised he had spoken to her that way, at that time of silence, that she nodded once: a single confirmation. He pivoted his head, and walked with swift, silent steps along the maroon carpet into the vestibule, and was gone.

Steve Kilduff sat staring out through the heat-vapored window of the coffee shop in downtown Sebastopol, watching the rain fall silver and heavy and then turn into flowing brown rivers, as if it had somehow become contaminated upon touching earth and concrete. To the west, over the roofs of the buildings, he could see an occasional jagged flash of lightning illuminate the leaden afternoon sky. Drum-rolls of thunder edged closer, grew louder, only moments apart now. When the gods are angry, mortals die, he thought foolishly; he shook himself and looked back to the cup of hot coffee which a pretty waitress had set before him. He began to stir a third cube of sugar into it.

Across the Formica-topped booth table, Larry Drexel set fire to a cheroot and watched him through the ensuing miasma of heavy smoke. He said at length, "That was a goddamned silly thing you did at the mortuary."

Kilduff laid his spoon very carefully on the saucer. "I suppose it was."

"Why, Steve?"

"I don't know," Kilduff answered. "Jim and I were . . . oh Jesus, Larry, we were friends once, good friends—you know that. I *had* to say something to his wife. I felt . . . Well, I had to, that's all."

"She didn't know us from a gnat's ass," Drexel said. "We were just faces at a funeral. But you had to go and wax emotional."

"She's not going to remember me."

"You'd better hope not."

"It's not that important, Larry."

"Everything's important now."

"Look, if it bothers you that much, why did you come to the funeral in the first place?"

"Because you insisted on coming," Drexel said. "Because you're emotional, and you react without thinking. Christ knows what you might have said to Conradin's wife later on if I hadn't gotten you away from there."

"I wouldn't have said anything to her."

"No? How do I know that?"

"Do you think I'm still a kid?"

"You act like a kid sometimes."

"Shit," Kilduff said.

"Yes, shit," Drexel said. He leaned across the table and put his face close to Kilduff's. "You wouldn't listen to me Saturday night. You wouldn't even consider what I said. You tried to pass the whole thing off as some pipe dream, because you were too weak and too afraid to admit to yourself that the past has finally caught up with us, that somebody wants us dead. Now tell me that isn't the way it was."

"The whole idea is . . . fantastic," Kilduff said slowly.

"That's right. It's fantastic. But what do you say now, baby? Do you think Conradin fell off that cliff accidentally Sunday night, like yesterday's papers had it? Four of us now in less than a month. Do you still call it coincidence?"

No, Kilduff thought, and he knew that it wasn't, that he'd known it wasn't almost from the beginning. He'd been deluding himself, lying to himself that there was nothing wrong, nothing to worry about; he just hadn't been able to face it. Too many things had happened at once, that was the reason—Andrea and the money and Granite City, all piling in on him at the same time. Was it any wonder he'd reacted the way he had? But he had to face it now, he had no choice but to face it now. Yes, it was true all right, it was murder all right; Jim hadn't misjudged his footing in the fog and fallen accidentally off that cliff. Somebody had pushed him and somebody had deliberately murdered Cavalacci and Wykopf and Beauchamp—this Helgerman, this Mannerling guard who had suffered spinal damage as a result of Conradin's blow to the base of his neck those thousand years past . . .

He said, "I don't think it was coincidence, Larry. I don't think Jim or any of the others died by accident."

"You weren't so sure on the phone last night. You wouldn't talk about it."

"I'm sure now."

Drexel drew back against the red Leatherette of the booth and inhaled the cheroot and expelled twin streams of smoke through his nostrils. "Okay," he said. "You're sure now. What do you think we ought to do?"

"I don't know."

"No, of course you don't."

"Just what does that mean?"

Drexel smiled in his cold way. "I'll tell you what we're going to do. We're going to find Helgerman. That's the only thing we *can* do."

"Find him? How are we going to do that?"

"By starting at the source."

"You mean Granite City?"

"That was where he lived, wasn't it?"

"If he killed the others, and now Jim, he can't have done it from Granite City. We won't find him there."

"No, he's here now. In the Bay Area."

"Then—?"

"It's a place to start," Drexel said. "He could be based almost anywhere around here, and we'd only be kidding ourselves if we think we can locate him by canvass. So we begin at the beginning and work our way forward and try to trace him that way. I had a flight scheduled to Chicago last night. I canceled it because of Conradin, but as soon as I get back I'm going to make another reservation. For tonight."

"And me?"

"What about you?"

"Do you want me to go along?"

"You'd rather not, is that it?"

"I didn't say that."

"You didn't have to."

"Don't put words in my mouth."

"Is that what I was doing?"

Kilduff rotated his cup slowly in its saucer, thinking: No, that's not what you were doing at all. You were right, Larry: I'm afraid. Because with acceptance comes fear, and I'm afraid the same way I was before we held up that armored car—maybe more so now, because I had youth then and all I've got now are a lot of old memories and faded dreams and the prospect of a life alone. I don't particularly want to die, but it's not death itself that I'm frightened of; no, it's . . . something else, something less simple, less basic, something else . . .

He said uneasily, "Listen, Larry. What can we do even if we find

Helgerman? Buy him off? I don't have a pot any more; my share is gone."

Drexel was looking at him with incredulity. After a long moment he said softly, "Come on, baby. You're not that goddamned naïve, are you?"

Outside the window, the sky irradiated for a brief instant with a fresh zig-zag of lightning, as if a gigantic match had been struck somewhere in the heavens, and then grew dark and ominous again. Kilduff's eyes flicked there briefly, came back to Drexel's. A chill began to flow through him.

"Naïve?" he said. "I don't—"

"What do you think we've been talking about? Taking him to dinner and a movie?"

"Larry—"

"What the hell do you *suppose* we're going to do when we find him?" Drexel said. "We're going to kill the bastard. We're going to kill him before he kills us."

The Tenderloin by night, as seen through heavy rain.

San Francisco's equivalent to New York's West Forty-second Street, on a smaller scale but nonetheless squalid, nonetheless garish, hiding its pocked and ugly face beneath the veiling rain and the cosmetic darkness, dying by inches and without mourners. A whore under every street lamp and two behind every drawn shade; gay-boys with mascaraed eyes and codpieces and invitational glances more sultry than those of their female counterparts; con men with sad eyes and glib tongues and hearts of pure ebony; pushers selling furtive oblivion in white capsules or brown packages or dabbed lightly on sweet sugar cubes; winos with nowhere to go and a future as dead as the past, suffering the penultimate indignation of having to compete with bearded and buckskinned hippies for altruistic nickels from Des Moines or Miami or the Sunset District—and here and there, a man who wants nothing and takes nothing and asks only to be left alone.

On Ellis Street, neon flashes AUGIES PLACE, sans apostrophe, alternately with TOPLESS AND BOTTOMLESS REVUE above a black-façaded building situated between a Polish delicatessen and an empty storefront decorated with chalked obscenities. A thick-necked man with a Fu Manchu mustache and flat drugged eyes stands before the curtained entranceway, calling out inducements to the stream of passers-by, "No cover and no minimum, folks," but he says nothing of the diluted bar whiskey which sells for a dollar fifty a shot and tastes like nothing so much as crude fuel oil.

Inside it is very dark, save for a single light above the back bar and a bright pink spotlight which illuminates a small, raised stage against the far wall. On the stage, a nude red-haired girl with pendulous white breasts and swollen nipples and a shaved, protruding abdomen makes lewd motions with fleshy hips, while an unintelligible masturbation of sound spews forth from a hidden jukebox. Before a chrome-barred cocktail slot stands a platinum-haired waitress wearing a brief sequinned halter and a short skirt with fringe ringing its bottom, and behind the otherwise empty bar a huge, light-skinned Negro sits on a high accountant's stool and surveys the almost deserted interior with implacable eyes.

Only three of the two dozen tiny round tables—which cover with their chairs every available inch of floor space—are occupied. At one, a sailor in dress blues and a hooker in a green lamé dress sit holding hands and whispering; at a second, two more hookers in shimmering black, waiting, silent.

At the third table sits the limping man.

He holds a glass of draft beer tightly between his two hands, and stares with hot brightness at the red-haired girl on the stage. He watches her hips undulate in time to the pagan music, simulating the act of love, her eyes squeezed shut and her lips half-parted in an expression of abandonment, and while he watches he thinks of Sunday night and Yellow.

So simple it had been, so very simple, simpler even than Red and Blue and Gray. Yellow, Yellow, true to form, the habitual animal: a walk along Blind Beach, like so many walks before. So simple. He had known Yellow's destination from the moment he turned onto Highway 1, and he had slowed down then and driven leisurely, for there was no need to remain near, and when he had finally taken the rented car onto the turn-out high above the ocean, Yellow's car had been parked there where it always was. So simple. So simple to hide in the fog on the ledge, to blend into the roiling eddies of mist and wait for Yellow to climb back up the face of the cliff after his walk and pause there, unsuspecting, so simple to reach out and very quickly thrust him into nothingness . . .

A movement, a thin rustling sibilance, diverts the limping man from his thoughts. He takes his eyes reluctantly from the girl on the stage. One of the hookers in shimmering black has come to his table, and she stands now above him, smiling, tall and willowy and young, with black hair piled high on her head, with breasts that spill like white iridescent cream over the tight bodice of her dress. "Do you mind if I sit down, honey?" she asks in a voice as sibilant as the rustle of her garment.

The limping man looks up at her for a long moment. A whore, a cheap whore; but he feels hunger in his loins. "No," he answers slowly, "I don't mind."

The girl sits down and crosses her legs, and the short skirt of the dress pulls up on her thighs: more iridescent white cream. His eyes linger there, and he can smell her perfume dark and musky. "I'm Alice," she says.

"Hello, Alice."

"Would you like to buy me a drink?"

"All right."

"Well, groovy."

"What would you like?"

"Bourbon and water."

The limping man signals and the yellow-haired waitress moves toward them, her heavy thighs rippling beneath the dancing fringe of her skirt. She takes his order and returns to the bar, and Alice says, "What's your name, honey?"

"Smith," the limping man answers, and Alice laughs. A cheap whore, he thinks, but she's almost pretty when she laughs.

"Where you from, old Smith?" Alice asks.

"Everywhere," the limping man says. "And nowhere."

Alice laughs again. "My, how poetic." She puts her hand on his thigh very lightly and leans close to him and presses her white spilling breasts against his arm. "You wouldn't be a poet, would you?"

Her hand is like hot fire on his leg. "No, I wouldn't."

"What would you be then?"

The limping man does not answer, and the yellow-haired waitress comes back with a tray containing a draft beer and a glass of tea. The limping man gives her three dollars. She nods, retreating. Alice sips the tea, and then puts the glass down and presses her breasts tighter against his arm. He feels them spongy-soft there and looks down into the shadowed valley between them and begins to breathe unevenly.

The music builds to a crescendo from within the walls of the room, and the red-haired girl moves faster and faster on the stage, until her nude hips are a blur of motion. Alice strokes the limping man's thigh, drawing her hand higher. "Do you like me?" she asks.

"Yes," he answers, "I like you," and he is thinking of Yellow again, Yellow screaming through the gray, damp fog.

"I've got a room down the street, honey," Alice says softly. "We could go there if you like."

Yellow screams and screams, but rhythmically now, in time with the beat of the music. The limping man breathes rapidly, irregularly, and her hand sets fire to his trouser leg.

"I'm very good, you know," she says.

"Are you?"

"I'm very, *very* good."

"How much?"

"Fifty dollars."

"That's a lot of money."

"I'm a lot of woman, honey."

"I'll give you twenty-five."

"Compromise time," she says. "Thirty-five."

"Twenty-five or nothing."

"Thirty-five or nothing."

The music continues, but the scream ends abruptly and is replaced by a faint, faraway sound, the sound of a pebble tumbling down a mountainside. But then that sound, too, dies, and there is silence, and in his mind the limping man sees Yellow lying dead and broken and bloodied at the bottom of the cliff. Alice's hand brands his thigh and she breathes into his ear, "I know a lot of things, old Smith honey, I know a lot of ways to make a man happy. Thirty-five dollars is a bargain price."

"All right!" the limping man says urgently, standing. "All right, let's go!"

Alice smiles. "You won't be sorry."

"Let's go!" he says again, and pulls her to her feet. They make their way quickly toward the curtained entranceway.

Behind the bar, the light-skinned Negro watches them with his implacable stare, and smiles very faintly, and on the stage the nude girl dancer sinks to her knees with her head hanging down and her long red hair shielding her body like a gossamer cloak as the music terminates and the pink spotlight winks out.

Chicago lay cold and bright and aloof under a darkly overcast sky when Larry Drexel's flight from San Francisco arrived at O'Hare Airport a few minutes past ten Tuesday night.

Immediately after claiming his single suitcase, Drexel entered a cab in front of the main terminal and instructed the driver to take him to one of the larger downtown hotels, where he had made telephone reservations that afternoon. He settled back against the rear seat as the cab began to make its way out of the airport, removed a cheroot from his suit pocket, and lit it carefully.

He thought: Who would have figured Kilduff to turn out the way he did? Crap-yellow, and running scared. He came undone at the seams this morning at Sebastopol; I shouldn't have said anything to him at all about killing Helgerman, but how could you predict a reaction like that?

It turned his stomach remembering how he had had to patronize Kilduff: "It's nothing as relatively unimportant as exposure, or even a prison sentence, facing us now, Steve. It's life and death, kill or be killed—the law of the jungle. No judgments, no great moral decisions, Steve; kill or be killed, pure and simple." But he'd finally gotten him calmed down on the drive back to San Francisco, telling him that they would talk it all out again when he got back from Chicago; but there was no figuring how long it would be before Kilduff got to thinking on the thing and made some damned-fool move that would blow the whole scene—like going to the police, spilling his guts . . .

He couldn't let that happen. He had too many things going for him—El Peyote and Cantina del Flores, which he now owned one hundred percent as of Monday morning at 10:43—too many avenues opening up, each of them leading to golden rainbows, to allow one son of a bitch who didn't have the balls for justifiable homicide to queer it all. He had thought it all out very carefully on the plane, and the way he saw it, he had just one way to go. The idea of tracing Helgerman back to San Francisco really wasn't feasible, and he'd just be kidding himself if he actually thought he could determine his whereabouts that way; but if he could learn where Helgerman lived, where he called home now, then there was a good chance he could reverse the entire situation. Helgerman would have to come home eventually, wouldn't he?

And when he did, then *he* would become the hunted and Larry Drexel would become the hunter.

As for Kilduff . . . well, he had made his goddamned bed, hadn't he? He was approaching the deep end, no mistake, and it was a certainty that he was going over the edge before too long. There was the distinct possibility that Helgerman would get him before then, because he had gotten Cavalacci and Wykopf and Beauchamp and Conradin; but there wasn't any assurance of that. And suppose Helgerman made a try and failed? Kilduff—straight to the fuzz for sure.

So he couldn't afford to take the risk—he couldn't afford to wait. The thing to do was fly back to San Francisco tomorrow sometime, whether or not he located Helgerman's address, because he could always return to Chicago and Granite City again. Get Kilduff alone somewhere, like he should have done before he left. Just the two of them.

And then hit him on the head.

Eliminate the threat once and for all.

Drexel moistened his lips, staring out at the flickering lights of the Windy City. He didn't much care for the idea of that, not really; they had been friends once and there was the chance Kilduff would straighten up, you never knew. But the odds were all wrong, and friendships meant nothing when it came to your own ass. He would do it, all right; there was no other choice in the matter. You had to protect yourself, didn't you?

Well, didn't you?

9

Trina Conradin lay with her eyes open wide in the canopied antique bed she had shared with her husband, in the big white house on Bodega Flat, and listened to the wind and the rain and the sounds of night, and asked God again and again, silently, rhetorically, why her husband had died. She lay without moving, the cool white sheets pulled up tightly to her throat, waiting for the momentary respite of sleep, waiting in vain for sleep that never came. All that came were ghosts, ethereal wraiths fluttering, whispering, playing tag along the high ceilings and within the old dark walls. And she couldn't cry any more; she couldn't cry.

At the first pale, filtered light of morning—what day? Wednesday?—the storm abated; the wind grew tranquil and the thunder ebbed into nothingness and the sound of the rain was very gentle on the glass panes of the window. Trina lay in the warm, empty bed and tried to imagine her future. What would she do? Where would she go? There were too many memories, too many ghosts, in this big old house—and in Bodega Bay. Sell the house, then, and sell Jim's boat and go away somewhere. To live alone somewhere, alone . . .

She pushed the thoughts away; not now, she told herself, this isn't the time. She slid out of bed, and dressed in a pair of old black capris and a gray pullover sweater, and went downstairs to the kitchen.

Shortly past eleven, Mr. Spencer, from the mortuary, arrived solicitous and apologetic to present Trina with a thin black leather-bound book which had *Inscribed Memories* printed in gold leaf on the cover. He took her hand and held it for a brief moment, as if it were a fragile sparrow's egg, and offered once more his whispered condolences. When he had gone, Trina sat in one of the dated wing chairs in the dark sitting room and opened the book and looked at the facing page. In raised black script:

That the memory
Of the beloved departed
May always be preserved,
We have compiled
This book of Inscribed Memories.

We present this record to you
In appreciation of your confidence and
As a tribute to your loved one,
Who will
Linger in fond remembrance throughout
The years to come.

On the page following, in the same printing, and handwritten carefully with a nibbed pen:

In Memory Of
And on the page following:

Entered into Rest
Sitting there, Trina still was unable to cry. She turned the parchment-like pages of the book in her lap slowly until she came to one divided into two columns, one headed: *Friends;* the other: *Relatives.* So few, she thought, so very, very few. Her eyes moved slowly down each column and then paused on the last signature under *Friends:* Steven Kilduff, San Francisco. She tried to place the name, to remember if she herself knew it from some past place or time, or if Jim had mentioned it, but it was totally strange and evoked no response in her mind. Steven Kilduff. Had that been the man who had spoken to her in the mortuary yesterday? Or was it the name of the other man, the dark Latin one? Why had only one of the two men signed the guest book in the vestibule? Why—?

Oh God, what difference does it make? Trina thought abruptly. She closed the memorial book. What difference does any of it make now—Jim's dead, Jim's dead, and everything else is meaningless.

She stood and went upstairs and put the book on the small reading stand by the bed. Then she descended again and entered the library—a small room with three walls of glassed-in bookshelves—just down the hall from the sitting room. She had to find something to do, something to keep her hands and her mind occupied . . .

Trina crossed to the roll-top desk and sat down in the stiff-backed armchair before it. Jim had handled all the financial responsibilities, by mutual consent, and she knew nothing about such things, really, having been given a budgeted allowance each week for food and incidentals. But she would have to learn; she would have to learn a lot of things now. She rolled the top up. Chaos—Jim had not been the most organized of men. Trina began to wade through the assortment of pigeon-holed, spindled, and stacked papers.

Twenty minutes later, she found the safe deposit key.

It was in a small locked steel strongbox in a locked bottom drawer of the desk. She had opened the drawer with a key on Jim's ring, which the Sheriff's Department had returned to her on Monday with the remainder of his personal effects, and which she had subsequently put in a small tray on the desk. There was nothing else in the drawer save for a new supply of checks from their joint account, and two boxes of canceled checks. The strongbox—for which she located a little silver key on the ring—contained, among other papers, their insurance policy, the deed to the house, ownership certificates on Jim's boat, *The Kingfisher*, and their marriage license; and it contained as well the safe deposit key, in an envelope with a series of yearly payment receipts from the West Valley Savings and Loan in Santa Rosa. The newest receipt was dated June, 1970, and she noticed that it was made out in both their names.

Trina held the key, Number 2761, in the palm of her hand. She remembered, a long while past, signing a paper from the bank on a safe deposit rental; Jim had said something vague at the time about keeping important documents there. She frowned. All the documents of any import were right there in the strongbox. Why had Jim then kept the safe deposit all these years, paying the rental promptly when it fell due? What did he have inside?

Unaccountably, Steve Kilduff found himself thinking about the day he and Andrea met.

February, 1963; he had been back in California almost a year, then, with the money in seven different San Francisco banks and a deal in the works with an operator named Thalinger, who was forming a combine to purchase virgin timberland for development near the Salton Sea in Southern California. It was practically an unprecedented coup, according to Thalinger, guaranteed to turn all the shareholders into rich men inside of five years—hell, it simply couldn't miss. Except that it did, by a sour mile, and he had lost two thousand in faith money. But that wasn't until later, after he and Andrea had met.

At the time, he was spending a couple of weeks at a ski lodge in Sugar Pine Valley in the Sierras, just taking it easy while the thing with Thalinger simmered, looking for willing pussy and not having any trouble finding it, living the good life, getting his. This one day, a Saturday, he'd been up on one of the intermediate slopes, trying half-seriously to get a big lemon-haired chick named Judy to ball him in a snowbank—"What the hell do you mean it's too cold? Eskimos do it in an *igloo*, don't they?"—and not having any luck at all, but enjoying himself immensely. He had come down to the lodge finally and put his skis up and crossed the ice-slick parking lot under the thin powder that had fallen all morning. There was a café in a big log building opposite, at the base of a slope where fifteen or twenty cabins nestled, smoke curling up through the brick chimneys on a couple of them, freezing white when it touched the chill air, and the whole thing had reminded him of a tranquil Christmas-card scene. He had got up onto the log-railed porch, whistling, when he looked through the rimed plate-glass window on the left and saw her sitting in one of the booths with a tall, blond guy in a fur-lined parka. She had her ebon hair down, falling across her shoulders and around onto her chest like silk, and her cheeks were a cherubic pinkish-red from the warmth inside, and she was smiling with her head cocked a little to one side, and the Scandinavian ski sweater in white and black that she wore was pulled tight across her small, round breasts as she leaned forward to listen to what the blond guy was saying.

He stopped and stood there on the porch for a long moment, with the snow falling around him and his breath making little puffs of vapor on the cold air, staring at her frankly and openly, and finally she seemed to become aware of his eyes through the glass and lifted her head and looked at him briefly, the smooth skin of her forehead wrinkling into two thin horizontal lines and the smile turning quizzical, lingering; but then she looked back to the blond guy again, and in his mind it was as if she had forgotten him, negated his existence with that simple averting of her eyes, and he went to the door and opened it and walked in and went straight to the booth and stood there looking down at her.

"My name is Steve," he said. "Steve Kilduff."

Her forehead wrinkled again, and the same quizzical, curious smile came onto her pink lips. "Hello," she said uncertainly.

The blond guy looked up at him with open hostility. His cheeks were pinkish-red, too, but on the table were two empty hot-buttered-rum mugs from the café's connecting bar, which had more to do with his color than the interior warmth. His eyes had a faint opaqueness, the whites interwoven with crimson lines. He said, "Flake off, McDuff."

"*Kil*duff."

"Whatever the hell," the blond guy said. "Flake off."

He kept looking at her, at her great luminous black eyes. "What do *you* say? Do you want me to leave?"

"I . . . don't know," she answered. "I don't know you."

"I'm Steve," he said. "Steve Kilduff, from San Francisco."

"Listen," the blond guy said, "nobody invited you. This is a private discussion."

"Oh, Kjel," she said. "Don't be like that." And to him, "I'm Andrea Fraser; and this is Kjel Andersson," smiling.

"Oh, a Swede," he said.

"What the hell do you mean by that?" Andersson asked hotly.

"I didn't mean anything by it."

"No?"

"No."

"Please, Kjel," she said. "Don't make a scene."

"For Christ's sake!" Andersson said, looking at her. "Whose side are you on?"

"I'm not on anyone's side."

"Tell *him* not to make a scene, then."

"*He* isn't raising his voice," she said, and there was the barest hint of anger in her tone now.

"Well, maybe you'd like *me* to flake off."

"Yes, maybe I would."

"All right, then, goddamn it!" Andersson said petulantly and slid out of the booth and glared angrily at Kilduff. He stalked to the door and went out.

He looked down at her and said very softly, "Would you mind if I sat down with you, Andrea?"

"Well . . . no, I guess not."

He sat down and kept looking at her, tasting her with his eyes, and inside him there was a paradoxical mixture of feelings old and new, intermingling as one: he felt an intense surging in his loins of sheer physical desire—he wanted her, he wanted her body as he had never wanted the body of any other woman; and yet he was consumed equally by a kind of fatherly-brotherly selfless knight-errantry that in itself precluded physical contact.

He said, "Listen, is Andersson anything to you?"

"What do you mean?"

"Fiancé or boyfriend, like that?"

"No, he's just a fellow I work with. At Prudential Life, in Oakland. We came up last night as part of a group, on a chartered bus for the weekend; but Kjel drinks too much, he really does, even this early in the day, and—"

He leaned forward. "Will you have dinner with me tonight?"

She blinked. "Pardon me?"

"Will you have dinner with me tonight?"

"Well, I . . ."

"There's a roadhouse a couple of miles from here," he said. "You buy your steaks by the pound and cook them yourself over wood charcoal. Do you like jazz? Gutbucket, with a lot of soul horn?"

"Yes, but . . ."

"We can go to Richie's afterward, on Interstate 40. It's a wild place. When you walk in, you feel like you've regressed forty years, to Bourbon Street in the twenties, if you know what I mean. What do you say, Andrea? Seven o'clock?"

She touched the tip of her tongue to her lips, and held it there, as a cat will do sleeping, and her eyes locked with his, probing, touching, and after a very long time—unsmiling now, eyes still locked—she said softly, "Yes, seven o'clock, Steve."

They were married in San Francisco five weeks later . . .

Kilduff lay on the unmade bed in the Twin Peaks apartment chain-smoking, with the hammered-bronze ashtray balanced on his chest, reliving it as vivid as yesterday, hearing her voice, seeing her so perfect and so innocent sitting there in the booth; and that night, all in soft blue ski clothes, and the touch of her lips for the first time—sweet, chaste, trusting, warm; and later, in San Francisco, at the Top of the Mark and the Venetian Room and that little place in the Russian colony on Clement, music soft and lights soft and the feel of her in his arms; and still later, the first whispered words from his lips under a so-corny gibbous moon, "I love you, Andrea," and her reply, breathless, a little awed, "Yes, oh yes, Steve, and I love you!"

Halcyon days, the days of wine and roses . . .

Viciously, now, Kilduff ground out his cigarette in the bronze ash-tray and swung his feet down and went into the kitchen. All gone, all dead, long dead—Jesus, why am I thinking about her like this? Why now, especially why now? He opened the refrigerator, a mechanical gesture, and looked inside: full larder, full to overflowing. She'd probably gone shopping before she left; that was the way Andrea was—walk out with a man's guts in her hands, dripping, but make sure he has enough food in the refrigerator. He slammed the door, turning.

Andrea, Andrea, I need you.

He stopped. No! Goddamn it, Kilduff, no, it's over, it's finished; she ran out, didn't she? The money ran out and she ran out, you don't need her, she's destroyed your love, you don't need her, you—don't—need—her.

Into the living room. The drapes were drawn, and it was dark in there. The rain came down in a soft, steady cadence on the balcony outside, and the wind tugged gently at the weather stripping around the glass doors, calling out. He held his right hand up to his eyes, and the hand trembled; he let it fall and returned to the bedroom and lay on the bed again.

What am I going to do? he asked of himself silently—the same question he had been asking of himself since yesterday morning, since Drexel had revealed to him in that coffee shop in Sebastopol what he was planning. But there was no answer now, either. He was caught in a vise, in one of those medieval iron maidens, caught in the middle with only two ways to go, with only two choices, no more and no less.

The police.

Or a party to murder.

No middle road, no tightrope line—one or the other. But which one? Could he walk into the Hall of Justice and into the Detective Bureau and say, "I'm one of the six men who robbed the Smithfield Armored Car in Granite City, Illinois, eleven years ago," could he walk in there and say that? But could he condone murder, passively allow Drexel to kill Helgerman in cold blood even though it was Helgerman's life or theirs? Yet he had to do one of the two, he had to make the decision, and soon, soon . . .

Suddenly, he sat upright on the bed with his heart plunging in his chest, and cold marrow fear, a different fear now, flowed through him like warm oil. Oh God! he thought, oh God! Because he didn't know if he *could* choose, he wasn't at all certain he *could* make that decision;

because there was an added dimension now, you see, something he had refused to comprehend before; because he understood with cold, complete clarity why he had been thinking about Andrea and why he needed her in spite of his self-deception that he did not; because in that moment Steve Kilduff realized exactly what he had become.

The single word echoed and re-echoed in his mind.

Coward, coward, coward . . .

10

Four down.
Blue and Gray and Red and Yellow.
Two left.
Green and Orange.
Green.
Yes—Green.

Sitting at the small writing desk in his room at the Graceling Hotel, the limping man carefully replaced the orange folder in the second of the two ten-by-thirteen manila envelopes. He spread the green folder open on the glass surface of the desk and began to study its contents again. He took small sips from a glass of milk which one of the bell-boys had brought up, and made marginal notes from time to time on the ruled sheets of paper, and consulted the Mobile Oil Travel and Street Map.

A half hour passed, and it was almost noon. The limping man put the pen down, smiling a little. Very good, he thought, very, very good. He closed the green folder and put it into the envelope with the orange one, and then put both envelopes into the American Tourister brief-case. He stood and rubbed at his eyes with the backs of his hands, stretching. A sharp pain lanced along his left rib cage. Alice —lowering his arms—Alice of the soft moist melting eyes and the long, long carmine claws; Alice slut, Alice whore, but Alice had been oh-so-good. She had screamed for him, and she had earned her money.

Just like Sonja, in Evanston.

And Jocelyn, in Fargo.

And Amy-Lynn, in Philadelphia.

They had all earned their money.

Damned right they had.

The limping man locked the briefcase and placed it on the bed. He knew how he was going to handle Green. Yes, and Orange too. The methods were a little more dangerous, a little more daring, but the whole thing was almost finished now and time was becoming important. Green and Orange had to be dispatched quickly; if they learned of the deaths of the others, there was the chance that they would run. And then he would have to start all over again.

He put his coat on and picked up the briefcase and rode the elevator downstairs. Outside, the wind blew a misty spray of clean, sweet rain in from the Bay, and swirled and eddied rubble in the swollen gutters. The sky was the color of steel. He walked into the face of the wind, thinking carefully, planning precisely.

In a department store near Union Square, he bought two average-priced cotton sheets. In a neighborhood grocery store, he bought a gallon of apple cider and a roll of cellophane food wrap. There was one other item he needed, but he would pick that up on the way tonight.

He started back to the Graceling. Just before he reached it, he turned abruptly into a large restaurant. He ordered a ham steak with candied yams and pineapple; all the walking and all the thinking had made him ravenously hungry.

Trina Conradin arrived shortly after two at the West Valley Savings and Loan, on Waycross Avenue in Santa Rosa. It was still raining, and the new wood and glass building looked sodden and cheerless against the gray backdrop of the sky.

Trina went in and crossed the marble floor to the safe deposit section. She signed her name on a slip of paper, and the girl in charge verified the signature with the card the bank had on file. A uniformed guard escorted her through the vault area, used his master key to open one of the two locks on Box Number 2761, and then carried the box to one of the small private cubicles along one wall. He put the box on the table inside, smiled pleasantly, and left her alone.

Trina sat down in the single chair and inserted the key she had found in Jim's desk into the second lock. She swung the hinged top upward, and looked inside.

And looked at money.

The box was jammed with it, in neat packets with a dun-colored currency wrapper around each one. There were packets of twenties, of fifties, of hundreds, crisp new bills, wilted old bills, filling the black metal container like a kind of wondrous and yet frightening green fungi.

Trina sat absolutely motionless, as if she had suddenly gazed upon Medusa and been turned into stone, listening to the funereal silence of the vault surrounding her and staring at the money. At first, she was unable to think; her mind became totally blank. But then, gradually, she began to come out of the mesmeric trance the money had momentarily put her in, and she thought: *Dear God, where did it come from, and it's real, it's real money, but where, Jim, where, how did you,* and she reached out to touch the top packet with the tips of her fingers. She pulled back again immediately, as if it were something unutterably alien.

She continued to stare at the money, and as she did she became aware of a yellowed edge of newsprint which was visible along one of the inner sides of the safe deposit box. She stared at that for a time, and then finally she reached out again and pulled it free.

It was a portion of the front page of the Chicago *Tribune,* folded in half, with the masthead showing and a date: March 16, 1959. She unfolded it and a black banner headline assailed her eyes:

$750,000 ARMORED CAR HOLDUP

And below that, over a three-column lead story, another black headline:

BANDITS MAKE SUCCESSFUL GETAWAY
IN DARING DAYLIGHT ROBBERY

And the story, prefaced by the words *Granite City, Illinois (AP):*

> Three masked men—half of what authorities believe to be a six-man gang—executed a daring daylight holdup of a Smithfield armored car near this western Illinois community early yesterday morning, eluding subsequent police roadblocks with more than $750,000 in cash . . .

Trina's hands began to tremble. A liquid opaqueness filmed her eyes and blurred the faded print. She blinked rapidly several times and read on with a kind of compulsive horror, her gaze moving slowly along the columns on the yellowed paper.

> Eyewitness observations lead police to believe that the two men

> who were responsible for planting the corrosive on the armored car's tire, and later assaulting Helgerman, were wearing theatrical make-up to alter their appearance in small ways. Inspector Yarnell stated, however, that such physical characteristics as height, weight, general build and eye color had not likely been changed.
>
> He described Bandit Number One as being a male Caucasian, 6'1, 180–190 pounds, in his early twenties, muscular build, medium complexion, greenish-brown eyes, soft-spoken. Bandit Number Two, the actual parking lot attacker of Helgerman, is also a male Caucasian, 5'10, 160–165 pounds, approximately the same age, lean build, deep-set gray eyes and long, thin nose . . .

Jim, Trina thought, that second man fits Jim's general description—and in that moment the full impact, all the implications, of what she was reading struck her and she pushed her chair back and came onto her feet, her eyes bulging wide and her mouth open and a terrible sick empty feeling in the core of her stomach.

"No," she whispered very softly, "no, no," and her eyes went back to the page section still held in her left hand. "No, please God, no," and another paragraph gathered and held her vision.

> Helgerman is reportedly in serious condition at Sisters of Mercy Hospital. The vicious blow which felled him, delivered to the base of the neck, might possibly have caused permanent spinal damage, according to the attending physician, Dr. Leonard Vacenti. "It's too early to tell, of course," Dr. Vacenti said, "but there exists the definite possibility that Mr. Helgerman may suffer mobility impairment of one type or another, ranging from minor locomotion difficulties to total paralysis . . ."

"No," Trina said, "no," and she flung the clipping from her. It fluttered down slowly, like a leaf in a gentle autumn breeze, oscillating to and fro until it touched the linoleumed floor; and then it lay still against one leg of the table. Not Jim, she thought, not Jim, not Jim; but the money stared up at her from the black metal box and the section of newspaper stared up at her from the floor, and they were both saying yes Jim, yes Jim, yes Jim.

She sank onto the chair again and stared at the door without seeing it. Armed robbery, vicious attack, a man possibly paralyzed for life—

and he had come home to her with enough money to marry, and to buy the big white house on Bodega Flat and the salmon fishing troller he had always dreamed of owning. Good man, kind man. Killer? Thief? No, no—but the time was right: March, 1959, and the place was right: Granite City, Illinois, just a few miles from Bellevue Air Force Station, and something had changed him, something had slowly taken him apart inside with a million cancerous teeth. Had that something been guilt? Was that the reason all this money—what was left after the house and the boat and the luxuries and the incidentals—had been allowed to lie dormant in the safe deposit box all these years? Had he been unable any longer to spend the blood spoils when the guilt became too strong? Wouldn't his complicity in this terrible crime explain why he had never been able to tell her what was troubling him, why he had kept it all bottled up inside him these long past years? Wouldn't it explain why he had refused to leave Bodega Bay, except when it was absolutely necessary, why he drank so much during the winter months when there wasn't the fishing to keep him occupied? Wouldn't it explain—

Why he had died?

God, God! Why *had* he died? Had his death really been an accident? Or—had it been something else?

Suicide? Had the guilt become too much for him to bear? Had he finally reached the breaking point Sunday night—and thrown himself off that high, fog-shrouded cliff at Goat Rock?

Or—

Murder?

No, not that, not that! Who would want to murder Jim? Unless . . . His partners? The other five men? But why would they want him dead? Why after eleven years? Who were they? Who—?

The two men at the funeral.

The two men sitting in the very last row at the mortuary!

Trina sat up very straight on the chair, and it was as if her body were encased in a block of glacier ice. The two men, one dark and Latin-appearing, the other tall and muscular. Tall and muscular. Greenish-brown eyes. Stopping to look toward her in the family alcove, soft-spoken—"Mrs. Conradin . . . I'm sorry, Mrs. Conradin"—Bandit Number One.

Steven Kilduff, San Francisco.

She stood up convulsively. The police. She had to go to the police. She had to tell them—

Tell them Jim Conradin had been a thief?

Tell them the man she loved had been a vicious criminal?

Hurt his family, hurt her family, destroy his name?

But she had to. If he had been murdered, his killers couldn't be allowed to go unpunished. And even if his death had been accidental, or suicidal, she couldn't live with the knowledge of his crime—she knew that—she couldn't live with it for one single day as he lived with it for eleven long years. She had to go to the police, she had to.

Jim, I have to, she thought, and she picked up the newspaper section from the floor and put it into the safe deposit box and swung the hinged lid closed. Jim, I have to, and may God have mercy on your soul and on mine for what I have to do; there's no other way.

She picked up the box—frightened, trembling, crying—and ran out of the cubicle.

11

Late Wednesday afternoon.

The phone rang at 4:55.

Kilduff came out of the kitchen where he had been making coffee and caught up the receiver on the second ring. There was the taste of chalk in his mouth. "Hello?"

"Steve? Larry."

"Yes?" tensely.

"I've got something."

Kilduff let breath spray almost inaudibly between his teeth. "Go ahead."

"Not on the phone."

"Christ, Larry—"

"Later," Drexel said. "Tonight."

"Where are you now?"

"Chicago. I'm booked onto the seven-thirty flight to San Francisco."

"Are you coming here?"

"No. My place. San Amaron Road in Los Gatos, Number 547. Can you find it?"

"I'll find it," Kilduff said. "What time?"

"The plane gets in at ten, Coast time. Give me better than an hour to get home. Say eleven-thirty."

"All right."

"Listen, Steve, is everything okay with you?"

"What do you mean?"

"You've been sticking close to your apartment?"

"Yes."

"You haven't talked to anyone?"

"Who would I talk to?"

"What about your wife?"

"I told you about her," Kilduff said. "She's gone."

"Okay, just stay cool."

"Sure."

"I'll see you tonight."

"Larry, what is it you've got?"

"Tonight," Drexel said. "Make sure you're there, Steve."

"Larry—" Kilduff began, but he was talking to a dead line.

He put the phone down and returned to the kitchen and looked at the coffee maker. The same painful constriction he had known on Saturday night was back in his chest, and his breathing had a nasal, labored quality. Well, what now? Had Drexel located Helgerman somehow? He'd sounded uptight on the phone, almost apprehensive, and that wasn't like him—always steady, always in command. Something was bugging him, bugging him heavy . . . Christ, Kilduff thought, suppose he's already found Helgerman? Suppose for some inexplicable reason Helgerman went home after he killed Conradin, and Drexel found him and . . .

Suppose he's already killed him!

I'd be an accessory before and after the fact, and wouldn't that make me equally as guilty as Drexel in the eyes of the law? Wouldn't that mean the gas chamber for me, too? The gas chamber—no, there weren't any more executions in California, were there? They only gave you life imprisonment now, life in a cage—what does it matter, anyway, because one is no more preferable than the other and there's no Statute of Limitations on the crime of murder—

The doorbell chimed.

Kilduff started, and a cold slimy thing attached itself parasitically between his shoulder blades. He sucked breath into his lungs like a gaffed fish. But then he rubbed a hand across his face and thought: Take it easy, now, just take it easy. No jumping at shadows, no reading malice into everyday sounds. Easy, son, easy. Hell, it was probably Mrs. Yarborough, the manager. He hadn't paid the rent for the month yet. Sure, Mrs. Yarborough. He went out to the foyer and pulled the door open.

Two men stood in the hallway outside. One was tall and thin, in his early thirties, with sandy hair immaculately combed and expressionless brown eyes and a chin that came to a long V-point. He wore a neat gray suit and a gray and white striped tie and a pale yellow button-down shirt with silver teardrop cuff links. The other man was shorter, older by ten years, but of the same leanness. He had a narrow, protracted nose that curved oddly, like a fishhook. He was dressed in a dark brown shiny-trousered suit, and in his left hand he carried an old brown hat with a torn sweatband.

The sandy-haired one said, "Mr. Steven Kilduff?" in a soft, almost mellifluous voice.

Kilduff looked at them and knew instantly who they were. He had an insane desire to fling the door closed, to turn and run, flee, run, run, but there was no place for him to go. The knot in his chest tightened until his lungs seemed to be rejecting the entrance of oxygen, and he tried to control the panic that was rising like a flood tide within him. It's something else, he thought, a traffic violation, something else; but he was lying to himself and he knew it. He put out his hand involuntarily against the door jamb, and washed saliva around in his mouth, and forced words past the dryness of his throat. "Yes, what is it?"

"My name is Commac," the sandy-haired one said. He brought his left hand up, and nestled against the palm was a leather case with a shield pinned inside. "Inspector Neal Commac, San Francisco police. This is my partner, Inspector Flagg."

His knees were suddenly jellied, and he knew the color had drained out of his face. He just stood there, holding onto the door jamb.

Commac watched him with his expressionless eyes. "Is something the matter, Mr. Kilduff?"

"No, I . . . no," Kilduff answered.

"We'd like to talk to you, please."

"About—what?"

"Inside, if you wouldn't mind."

He worked some of the saliva onto his lips. "No, of course not."

The two men came in past him and entered the living room. They stood with their eyes moving slowly over the interior, photographing it. Kilduff shut the door and went in there. "Well," he said, facing them, trying to get a smile on, trying to brazen it out, knowing that he wasn't even close to pulling it off, "sit down, won't you?"

"Thank you," Commac said, and they sat down on the sofa. Flagg put his hat on his knees, balancing it there.

"Can I . . . offer you anything? Some coffee?"

"Nothing, thank you."

Kilduff sat on one of the chairs opposite, leaning forward, and got a cigarette out of his pocket. He managed to keep his hand steady as he lit it. "What is it I can do for you?"

"You attended the funeral of James Conradin in Sebastopol on Tuesday, yesterday," Commac said. "That right, Mr. Kilduff?"

The urge to take flight came back on him, and he had to make a concentrated effort of will to throw it off. They know, he thought, somehow, in some way, they've found out and they know. All right, what do I do now? Do I tell them, admit it, get it done with? They have ways of dragging information out of you, they're professionals, cops, they know how to trap you into making admissions. I can't get away with lying to them, not for very long, not when they already know. All right, then, all right. All I have to do is confirm it, tell it straight, make it easy on myself, sure, no agonizing decisions to reach, no more sweat and no more fear, it's over and the choice has been made for me and all I have to do is confirm it . . .

"Mr. Kilduff?"

He came out of it. "What?"

"I asked you if you attended the funeral of James Conradin yesterday."

"I . . . yes, yes I did."

"Conradin was a friend of yours?"

"I knew him in the service."

"When was this?"

"From 1956 to 1959."

"You were stationed together?"

"Yes."

"Where?"

"The Bellevue Air Force Station."

"That's in Illinois, isn't it?"

"Yes."

Commac studied him for a long moment. Kilduff just sat there with his lips pressed tightly together and the cigarette curling smoke upward into the still air of the room. He couldn't do it. He couldn't do it, he couldn't say the words, he couldn't even meet Commac's eyes. He couldn't do it, not now and not later, and now was the time because Commac had already begun to probe, still playing along the surface, yes, but it wouldn't be long before he would penetrate deeper and deeper; now was the time and he simply couldn't do it.

"When was the last time you saw Conradin, Mr. Kilduff?" Commac asked. "Alive, I mean."

"It must have been . . . oh, eleven years ago," he answered, and that was the first lie. It came flowing out of his mouth like warm butter, without effort, without conscious consideration. And he knew the ones which would follow would be just as smooth and just as accomplished. "It was right after we were discharged."

"When was that?"

"February of 1959."

"And you hadn't seen him since that time?"

"No."

"Did you know he lived in Bodega Bay?"

"Before I heard of his death, you mean?"

"Before then."

"No," Kilduff said. "No, I didn't."

"I see," Commac said. "Were you close friends in the service?"

"I . . . guess we were, yes."

"How is it you never kept in touch after you got out?"

"I don't know. People drift apart. You know how that is, Inspector."

"Uh-huh," Commac said.

Flagg took a stick of spearmint gum from the pocket of his brown suit, unwrapped it carefully and wadded the foil into a little ball and put the ball in the ashtray on the coffee table. He chewed with his mouth closed, quietly.

Kilduff thought with self-loathing and with self-pity: You goddamned coward, you goddamned frigging coward, you yellow gutless wonder—it's never going to be this easy again, if you can't do it now you'll never do it.

And he still couldn't do it.

Commac said, "Who was the other man, Mr. Kilduff?"

"What other man?"

"At the funeral with you on Tuesday."

"I don't know who you mean."

"You were sitting with a dark-complected man, Latin features, expensively dressed. Together, in the last row of chairs during the service."

"Oh, yes, that man," Kilduff said. "Well, I don't know his name."

"You just happened to sit by one another, is that it?"

"Yes, that's it."

"And you neglected to introduce yourselves."

"You don't usually observe the amenities at a funeral."

"Come on now, Mr. Kilduff," Commac said mildly. "You came in together and you sat down together."

"I told you, I don't know the man. I never saw him before yesterday. Listen, what's this all about? Why are you asking all these questions?"

Flagg continued to chew his gum quietly. He had begun to rotate his hat between his thumb and forefinger. Commac's expressionless eyes never left Kilduff's face. He took a small clothbound notebook from the inside pocket of his gray suit and opened it and studied a page. He frowned. "Bellevue, Illinois," he said. "That's near Granite City, isn't it?"

"Yes, it's near Granite City."

"That was where they had that big Smithfield armored car robbery," Flagg said, speaking for the first time. His voice was as soft as Commac's. "April of fifty-nine, wasn't it, Neal?"

"March," Commac said. "March 15th."

"Sure," Flagg said. "Six men got away with over seven hundred and fifty thousand in cash. They were never caught."

"No," Commac said, "they never were."

"Consensus seemed to be that it was an amateur job, the way it was pulled off," Flagg said. "Lacked the professional touch."

They were talking through him now, watching him, testing him for a reaction. Oh, they knew, all right. He hadn't had any doubt in his mind from the beginning. He sat there and tried to make himself tell them about Granite City, and about Drexel and Helgerman, but it was just no use.

Commac said, "Do you remember the Smithfield robbery, Mr. Kilduff? It made quite a splash in the Illinois papers."

"I remember it," he answered softly. "But I don't see what that has to do with Jim Conradin. Or with me."

"Maybe it has a lot to do with *him*," Flagg said carefully.

"Are you saying Jim was mixed up in that?" Kilduff tried to make his voice incredulous, but the words came out flat and toneless.

"There's a good chance of it," Commac said. "A very good chance of it."

"How do you mean that?"

"Conradin's wife opened their safe deposit box this afternoon," Flagg said. "Up in Santa Rosa. What do you suppose she found in there?"

"I don't have any idea."

"Money."

"Money?" The incredulity was there this time, and genuine.

"Forty-one thousand and some-odd dollars."

"But that—"

"And a newspaper clipping," Commac said. "Dealing with the robbery."

"That doesn't prove Jim was involved."

"No, it doesn't. But just the same, it opens up a lot of possibilities, wouldn't you say?"

"Look, why come to me? I don't know anything."

"Mrs. Conradin remembers you from the funeral," Commac said. "She says you spoke to her at the mortuary."

"Well, so what?"

"That newspaper clipping I mentioned. It carried general descriptions of the only two bandits whose faces were seen."

"So?"

"They match both Conradin and you, Mr. Kilduff."

"For Christ's sake!" he exploded. "You just said they were general descriptions. I look like a million other guys, and so did Jim Conradin."

"Sure," Flagg said. "We know that."

"Do I strike you as some kind of hoodlum?"

"Nobody said anything about hoodlums."

"Who else would rob an armored car?"

"Six young guys who thought they had a foolproof scheme worked out," Commac said. "Maybe ex-soldiers, regimented and disciplined."

"What is it you're trying to say, Commac?" Kilduff asked. "That I was one of the six men? That Jim Conradin and I were both in on it? Is that it?"

"Were you?" Commac asked quietly.

Well, there it was. The question. No long speeches now, Kilduff. One word, that's all, just one word. *Yes*. Say it. Just open your mouth and say it. Say it, you son of a bitch!

Yes.

"No," he said. "And I resent your accusations."

"I'm not making any accusations, Mr. Kilduff."

"What the hell else would you call it?"

"You know," Flagg said softly, "if you *were* involved there's nothing we can do to you now. The Statute of Limitations ran out a long time ago."

"If I was involved, and I'm not, I'd still be a fool to admit it."

"Maybe so," Commac said.

"Listen, I don't know where Conradin got that money his wife found and I don't care. If he was in on that robbery, I never knew anything about it."

"All right, Mr. Kilduff," Commac said in a placating way. "Now, suppose you tell us a little more about Conradin."

He lit another cigarette from the butt of the first one. "Like what?"

"Do you remember the exact date of the last time you saw him?"

"No, I don't."

"Just like that? Without consideration?"

"I don't remember. It was after we were discharged."

"Then it was in February of 1959."

"Yes, February."

"And where was that?"

"I don't remember."

"Granite City?"

"No."

"I thought you didn't remember."

"Goddamn it, you're trying to confuse me!"

"Take it easy, Mr. Kilduff," Flagg said.

"Christ," Kilduff said.

"Can you give us the names of some of Conradin's friends?" Commac asked. "Other than yourself, that is."

"I don't remember."

"You don't remember any of his friends?"

"No."

"I thought the two of you were buddies?"

"We were."

"Well, all right. Then give us the names of some of your *mutual* friends."

I can't do it, Kilduff thought, I can't tell them, it's no use, and I'm going to pieces sitting here. I've got to see Drexel, I've got to talk it out with him, I've got to have some time to think. He got on his feet and stood there trembling. "I don't have to answer any more of your questions," he said. "You've got no right to come here like this and accuse me, and I don't have to answer any more."

They looked up at him impassively.

"Listen," Kilduff said, "if you think I'm some kind of criminal, why don't you arrest me? Why don't you take me downtown and book me and grill me in the back room? Isn't that the way you people do it?"

"No, that's not the way we do it," Commac said softly. "And we couldn't arrest you if we wanted to. You know that as well as we do. The Statute of Limitations has long since run out on the Smithfield robbery."

"Then what are you digging it up again for?"

"It's our job," Commac said simply.

"Well, I think you'd better leave now. I don't have any more to say to you."

They got to their feet in unison. Commac said, "I think you've said quite a bit already, Mr. Kilduff."

They moved unhurriedly to the door and Commac opened it and Flagg said, "We'll be in touch." They went out and Commac closed the door very softly behind them.

12

In his room at the Graceling Hotel, the limping man lay in darkness, his hands clasped behind his head, resting, thinking. Through the rain-streaked glass of the single window, he could see the coral-tinged light from some proximate but unseen neon sign blink on and off, on and off, on and off through the thinly falling night mist. Faint automobile sounds drifted through the panes and beneath the wood frame, muted, directionless.

The luminescent dial of his wristwatch read: 10:25.

Five minutes.

Everything was ready. He had all the items he needed—save for the one he would buy on the way—in a large, double-strength shopping bag with braided-twine handles. The Ruger .44 Magnum Blackhawk revolver was freshly oiled and freshly cleaned and freshly loaded, wrapped again in the chamois cloth at the bottom of the American Tourister briefcase. He wouldn't need it, of course; but it was there, and it was ready. Just in case.

He watched the greenish second hand of his watch sweep another minute away.

10:26.

In one hour, perhaps an hour and a half at the outside, barring difficulties unforeseen, Green would die.

And there would only be Orange.

The limping man smiled faintly in the darkness and swung his legs off the bed and sat up and gained his feet. He found his canvas shoes and put them on, and put on his overcoat, and lifted the shopping bag and the briefcase from the glass-topped surface of the writing desk. He went to the door and opened it and stepped out into the hallway and locked it behind him.

He looked at his watch again.
It was exactly 10:30.

Fran Varner stared at the telephone in the kitchen of her Santa Clara apartment, willing it to ring, willing Larry's voice to be on the other end, knowing that it wouldn't ring at all, waiting for a few more minutes to pass so that she could dial his number again for the twentieth or thirtieth time since six o'clock.

Thinking about the growing foetus deep in her womb.

She hadn't been able to put off seeing a doctor any longer; she had finally realized that yesterday. She had to know, one way or the other. She had made an appointment with a physician in San Jose whom she had once seen for a virus infection. Embarrassed and ashamed by the absence of a wedding band on her left hand, she had refused to meet the doctor's eyes during the consultation and the subsequent examination; but he had been very nice, and very kind, and very understanding. He wasn't there to make moral judgments, he had told her; that wasn't his profession—or his inclination. He would know the results tomorrow, he had told her. Call him at three.

She had called him at two-thirty, holding her breath as his nurse put the call through to him, telling herself the tests would prove negative, they simply had to prove negative . . .

And then he had come on the line and said quietly, "I'm sorry, Miss Varner, the Achheim-Zondek was positive. You are pregnant."

She had taken it very well, considering.

She had telephoned El Peyote immediately after promising the doctor she would come in for regular check-ups, and told Juano, who was managing things while Larry was away, that she wouldn't be in tonight—she had some kind of bug. Then she had gone home and thought it all through, weighing the alternatives.

How much did she love Larry Drexel? More than life itself, that was how much. But suppose he wouldn't marry her when she told him of the child? Suppose, as she had feared all along, he refused flatly? Did she want this baby—her baby, their baby—more than she wanted Larry?

No, she wanted nothing, no one, that much.

Then her recourses were clear.

Adoption.

Or abortion.

The latter was totally unthinkable. In spite of everything, she was incapable of committing a sin of that magnitude; if she had been unable to prevent the *conception* of human life by simply taking birth control pills, how could there be within her the capacity for *destroying* an unborn child, a child of and within her body, from the seed of the man she loved?

But adoption—yes, she would do that. It wouldn't be easy, especially if she saw the baby after it was born, if she held him (her?) in her arms, so warm and soft and defenseless; it wouldn't be easy, but she would do that if it meant keeping Larry. She would find a good foundling home where they screened the applicants very carefully, where only those who desperately wanted a baby and would give it love and a good home and all the requisite material benefits, too, were allowed to adopt, and if necessary she would do it out of her money. Of course that wouldn't be necessary, because Larry wasn't a cruel man—strange and cold at times, but never cruel; he wasn't like those men you read about in books who got a girl in trouble and then denied all responsibility and abandoned her completely. Not Larry, not her Larry.

Why, she might even be wrong about his refusal of marriage.

He might *want* to marry her with the baby coming.

There really was a good chance of that.

There really was.

She had to see him, she had to tell him about the child in just the right way. And she had to do it soon, very soon.

She called El Peyote again, but Juano didn't know where he had gone—"back east somewhere, I think, he didn't say exactly"—and he didn't know when Mr. Drexel would be back. Yes, he would have Mr. Drexel call her as soon as he showed up there, yes, no matter what time it was, yes, he would tell him it was urgent.

Fran had begun calling his home then, just before six, and it was ten-fifty now. No answer yet, and her phone had not rung. She continued to stare at the instrument, and she imagined she could feel the child move inside her. She closed her eyes and put one hand against her abdomen, pressing it there; then she opened her eyes again and with her other hand lifted the receiver out of its cradle, put it down on the breakfast bar, dialed Larry's number again, and then picked it up and put it to her ear. She listened to it ring five times, six, seven, eight . . .

Then: "Yeah, hello?" a little breathlessly.

Her hand tightened around the receiver, and she leaned forward, her heart singing violently in her chest. "Larry? Oh, thank God!"

"Fran?"

"Yes, darling," she said. "Oh, Larry, I . . ." The words constricted in her throat, and she swallowed and tried again. "Larry, I have to see you."

"Sure, baby," he said. His voice was distant, abstracted. "Tomorrow, at El Peyote."

"No, no, tonight."

There was a brief silence. Then he said, "Look, Fran, I just got in from Chicago. It's late, and I'm tired . . ."

"Larry, I have to see you!"

"No."

"Please, please, I have to!"

"Goddamn it, I told you no."

"Darling, please, it's . . . it's very important."

"I don't give a crap how important it is," he snapped. "Not tonight. Do you understand? Not tonight!"

He hung up.

Fran replaced the receiver very carefully. Her eyes were like polished amber pebbles glistening in a thin rain. She felt warm moisture begin to flow high along her cheekbones, and she put up her hands with the palms turned outwards to wipe it away—the gesture of a pigtailed little girl scolded for mud-pie batter on a pink organdy dress.

But she wasn't a little girl any more, oh no, not now, especially not now; what she was, was a consummated woman, carrying the illegitimate child of her lover in her womb, and the sooner she faced that, the better it was going to be for her, and for Larry, and for her unborn daughter or son. It was certainly time for her to assume the responsibility of her situation, to take some initiative in seeing it through this primary crisis, instead of merely lying back all dewy-eyed and trembling and innocently passive. She took her hands down and drew in several deep breaths, and her mouth firmed into a tight, resolute line. Yes. Yes, it was certainly time.

She thought: You're the father of my baby, Larry, and you have to know that, for better or for worse, and you have to know it now, tonight. It's the wrong time, perhaps—you're tired and you're in a poor humor and I'm more afraid now than ever of what you'll say when

I tell you—but I can't wait, I just can't wait, not until tomorrow, not this night through. I have to tell you, I'm going to tell you. I am.

She went into the bedroom and put on her plastic, belted raincoat and a matching, softly wide-brimmed rain hat. Then she left the apartment and went down the wood-and-fieldstone outer stairs to the parking area in the rear courtyard, running a little through the gentle rain to where her car was parked. She fumbled with her keys and got the door unlocked and slipped inside. She had a glimpse of the dashboard clock in the pale light from the ceiling dome just before she closed the door after her.

The time was 11:02.

Andrea Kilduff held the telephone receiver pressed tightly with both her small hands, listening to the distant, empty circuit noises humming through the earpiece. No answer.

On the fifteenth ring, she put the receiver back on its hook and shivered tremulously inside her heavy wool jacket. She hugged herself, and the wind moaned across the wet, puddled blacktop outside the glass walls of the public booth, fanning clumps of darkly painted autumn leaves toward the bright fluorescent lights of the Shell station at the opposite end of the rectangle. And there was the mournfully constant hissing of cars passing along the rain-slick expanse of Highway 101, near the first of the three Petaluma exits less than a thousand yards away.

Why didn't he answer? she asked herself silently. It's after eleven now; he should be home. He really should be home. Where would he be at this hour on a Wednesday night? He never goes to bars or anything like that, and seldom to the movies, and he certainly wouldn't go walking in Golden Gate Park this late. Maybe he's . . . out with someone. Well, no, I don't think so. No, he wouldn't be, but he isn't home and he should be home.

Andrea retrieved her dime and dialed the apartment number again, carefully. She let it ring another fifteen times. Again, no answer.

Damn! Why hadn't she made up her mind to call him sooner? She'd been thinking about it all day, hadn't she?—she hadn't slept much at all last night thinking about it. And she'd known darned well that she was going to do it, because she simply had to talk to Steve; this way wasn't any good at all. She had to talk to him and get it all said and done with, say all the words she'd been afraid to say to him before: words like "divorce" and "property settlement" and "good-bye." She didn't want to say them, ever, they were like lashing epithets, but this way—her way—had been a fool's errand from the very beginning, a defense against those words but an ineffective one, only prolonging the inevitable. At long last, she was woman enough to admit that she had been wrong. And so she had driven here from Duckblind Slough, through the wind and the rain to the nearest telephone because the Miramonte Marina and Boat Launch was closed for the night; but it had been for nothing, Steve wasn't home . . .

A sudden thought struck her.

Suppose the reason he wasn't home was because he had moved out? Suppose he had packed up his things and gone—but where? To a hotel? To a new apartment? What if he had left San Francisco altogether? What if he had just run away? Oh God, how would she find him if that were the case?

Wait a minute now. Well, for crying out loud, if he *had* moved out, if he *had* gone away, the telephone would be disconnected, wouldn't it? Of course it would. That recorded voice would have come on and said, "I'm sorry, the number you have dialed is not in service at this time." Of course, don't be silly, Andrea, he's just . . . out somewhere for the evening, that's all, oh, but if he moved this morning or this afternoon, the telephone wouldn't necessarily have to be disconnected yet, maybe they couldn't get a man up to do that until tomorrow, maybe he really is gone . . .

Steve, she thought. Oh Steve!

She took her dime from the return slot again and slid it into the circular opening above and dialed the number of Mrs. Yarborough, the building manager. She had to know, she had to know right now. She held the receiver in both hands, as she had before, waiting, and through the wet glassed walls of the booth, across the puddled blacktop, she could see the wide-faced clock mounted on the wall above the door to the Shell station office.

The hands and the numerals, their luminosity eerily blurred by the rain-mist, designated the time as 11:10.

The rain fell heavily, in a diagonally silver cascade, on the James Lick Freeway just below Candlestick Park. The onrushing yellow headlamp eyes of the northbound traffic, the desperately flashing blood-red taillights on the southbound automobiles strung out ahead, commingled to form a kaleidoscopically distorted montage—surrealism in motion, a wild hallucinogenic excursion into the depths of a nightmare.

This is the Twilight Zone, Steve Kilduff thought inanely, detachedly; enter Rod Serling on a fade-over with his soporific voice explaining the intricacies of the plot . . .

Off on his left, the black moving water of the Bay stretched cold and lonely on a flat plane toward the jeweled but half-obscured lights of the East Bay. The wind blew and whistled in a kind of ghostly charivari at the slightly open wing window, the windshield wipers worked in hypnotic metronome cadence on the rain-drenched glass, and the treble voice of a disc jockey on the too-loud radio sent discordant vibrations of sound echoing through the car—all serving to heighten the sense of unreality which pervaded Kilduff's mind.

He sat stiffly erect, with his hands clenching the wheel tightly and the muscles cording in his forearms. He had left Twin Peaks just before eleven, driving mechanically. He had been thinking only of Drexel; and what it was Drexel had found out, or had done, in Granite City; and what Drexel would say when he told him about Commac and Flagg—the two polite, soft-spoken cops who knew; and what Drexel would decide their next move to be; yes, and how he, Kilduff, would end up going along with it whatever it was.

Green and iridescent-white exit signs appeared, and then vanished, in the hazy aureoles of light from his head lamps.

GRAND AVENUE—SOUTH SAN FRANCISCO

SAN BRUNO AVENUE—SAN BRUNO

SAN FRANCISCO INTERNATIONAL AIRPORT

MILLBRAE AVENUE—MILLBRAE

BROADWAY—BURLINGAME

19TH AVENUE—SAN MATEO

HOLLY STREET—SAN CARLOS

WHIPPLE AVENUE—REDWOOD CITY

When would this phantasmagoria that was an all-too-real reality end? he asked himself as he sent the car hurtling along the rain-swept highway. How long would it be before the law of averages caught up with him? He was living on borrowed time, walking on eggshells, balancing on a mile-high tightrope, there was no way he could possibly come out of it unscathed; there was no way, simply no way, he could ever return to the former status quo security.

The radio disc jockey announced the time just as EMBARCADERO ROAD—PALO ALTO loomed into view ahead.

It was 11:23 and thirty seconds.

13

11:28.

Larry Drexel poured himself another glass of *aquardiente,* his third since he had arrived home, and resumed his restless pacing of the parlor's Navajo rug. The pallid light from a lantern-style wall lamp made his face look grotesquely demoniac, like a sculpted burlesque of an entity from Dante's *Inferno.*

Goddamn it! he thought, drinking from the glass, moving with long, fluid strides the width of the darkly somber room, turning at the fieldstone fireplace, retracing his steps, turning again. Where the hell was Kilduff? Sure, he'd told him eleven-thirty, but you'd think the bastard would—

Euphonious chimes echoed through the darkened house.

Reflexively, Drexel's hand went to the .38-caliber Smith and Wesson revolver in the side pocket of his suit coat. He touched the grip, and the feel of the cold, rough metal seemed to relax him. He took a slow breath, thinking: Easy, now, it's Kilduff and it's about time. But he went slowly, silently, along the front hallway and drew back the tiny round cover which guarded the peephole in the arched wooden door—no use in taking chances even if it was Kilduff, especially now . . .

But it wasn't Kilduff.

It was Fran Varner.

He pulled open the door, his nostrils flaring with sudden anger and splotches of crimson flecking his smooth cheeks. "What the hell are you doing here? I thought I told you I didn't want to see you tonight."

She took off her plastic rain hat and shook her brown hair. Her eyes probed his imperiously. "I have to tell you something, Larry," she said softly. "And it simply can't wait."

"The hell it can't! Go home, Fran . . ."

"No," she said. She held the rain hat clutched tightly in both hands, twisting it between her long, slim fingers. "No, I won't go home until I've talked to you."

Drexel thought: You silly, clinging bitch. "Listen," he said, "I can't talk to you now. Don't you understand that?"

"Why not, Larry?"

"I'm expecting someone."

"Who?"

"It's none of your business."

"Another girl?"

"Oh, Jesus!"

"Is it, Larry?"

"No, it's not another girl. It's business!"

"At eleven-thirty at night?"

He wanted to hit her. He wanted to lash out with his balled fist and knock her flat on her soft round little ass, teach her not to come around here bugging him like this when he was caught up in something so damned big, what the hell was the matter with these chicks? But he didn't hit her. He didn't hit her because Kilduff was going to arrive here any minute now and he had to get rid of her before then and he couldn't get rid of her if she was lying on her ass on the fieldstone walk.

He said in a cold, deliberate voice, "Fran, I'm telling you, if you know what's good for you, go home. Get out of here and go home right now. I mean it, Fran."

There was hurt and pain deep in her amber eyes now, as if she had just fully accepted a great, sad truth—not that he gave a crap what it was; all he cared about at that moment was getting rid of her. He thought she would obey his command, expected it with that hurt and pain in her eyes, but she caught him off guard. She said, "I'm coming inside, Larry," and before he could react she was past him and walking down the hallway into the parlor.

Rage welled up inside Drexel until the blood pounding in his ears sounded like a distorted drum-roll. He slammed the door savagely and went in after her. She had turned and was standing in front of the scrolled desk, her plastic raincoat dripping crystalline beads of water onto the rug. She waited until he had taken two steps into the parlor from the hallway, his eyes blazing, and then she said in a loud, clear voice, without preamble, "I'm pregnant, Larry. I'm going to have your baby."

It stopped him. It stopped him cold. His mouth opened, and then closed, and he stood there staring at her.

You bitch! he thought finally. I ought to kill you, you stupid little bitch!

11:28.

The street was half a block long, and ended abruptly in a white city barricade that stretched most of its width. To the left, facing in, was a densely grown area—a miniature wilderness—containing oak and eucalyptus and high grass and wild blackberry. To the right was a neatly trimmed green box hedge, jutting some ten feet thickly skyward, which fenced the property of some unseen and grandiose dwelling. Beyond the barricade was a short expanse of deciduous turf that formed a gradual down-slope leading to a narrow, meandering creek below.

The limping man parked the rented Mustang nose-up to the white barricade, shut off the lights and the engine, removed the key from the ignition, and stepped quickly out into the thinly falling drizzle. He went around to the rear and opened the trunk. He put on a pair of black pigskin gloves and worked swiftly there for something less than two minutes, darting occasional looks over his shoulder at the cross street, seeing nothing. Finally, he lifted from the trunk the double-strength shopping bag. He closed the deck lid and, carrying the shopping bag in the bend of his left arm, moved rapidly around the near end of the barricade.

He began to climb slowly, cautiously, down the slippery bank, with his free hand holding onto bushes that grew there, digging the heels of his canvas shoes into the spongy ground. After a time, he stood on the sharp stones at the edge of the creek bed. In its center, a narrow, shallow stream of rain water rushed past; the creek had been dry when he had last seen it, six weeks earlier.

The limping man rested there for a moment, and then started off to his left, walking slowly, cradling the shopping bag in close to his body. It was very dark. The sky was the color of soot, and the trees and bushes limned against it were little more than formless black shadows. He paused once, listening. There was no sound, save for the temperate fall of the rain and the sibilant rush of the creek water. The night was wet and black and silent around him—a huge enveloping blanket—and he was safely hidden within its folds. He moved forward again.

When he reached the half-upright log imbedded in the soil at the creek's edge, he stopped and peered across to the opposite side. He could see the wall there, a solid black line atop the bank, and he nodded once and began to pick his way gingerly across the bed. It was littered with leaves and twigs and mud and various bits and pieces of garbage carried and deposited by the accelerated rain water. The footing was treacherous, but he reached the opposite bank without incident.

He began to work his way upward along its surface. The contours of the stone-and-mortar wall became evident to him, and then he was standing before it, with his left hand steadying his body on the cold, moist stone. He could not see over the top of the wall from that point. He went to a build-up of silt on a higher section of ground near the far end of the wall. From there he was able to peer cautiously over the top at what lay beyond it.

An elongation of pale light spilled out through a glass-enclosed archway in the house across the interior patio; it gave substance to the shapes within the patio. So Green was still up and about, the limping man thought. Well, all right. Better if he was asleep, but not really that important; he could come back later of course, but he was here now, and there was really no need in taking unnecessary chances.

Carefully, he placed the shopping bag on the flat top of the wall. He swung himself up by utilizing the power in his wrists and forearms, favoring his game leg; he was an agilely poised black shadow for an instant atop the wall, and then he dropped inside the patio, crouching on one of the *macetas,* listening. There was no discernible sound from within the house. He straightened momentarily to lift the shopping bag down, and after a few seconds he began to make his way slowly, silently, across the stone floor of the patio. He paused at the fountain in its center, by one of the stunted Joshua trees, unhurried now, moving with care, with precision.

He reached the wall beside the glassed archway and flattened himself against the damp stucco. His ears strained, and voices—faint, but comprehensible—filtered through the glass.

". . . are you going to do, Larry?"

Woman's voice. Green had company. Well, maybe she would leave, but he couldn't wait very long. If she was still in there when the time came, then that was too bad for her. Damned whore anyway, what did it matter? He couldn't afford to be humane, not now, not now.

". . . expect me to do?" Green's voice, harsh and cold.

"Marry me, Larry. That's what I expect you to do."

"Marry you?" Laughter, without humor. "Jesus! I told you to take the goddamned pill, didn't I? Is it my fault you're too stupid to do it?"

Silence. And then: "You . . . never loved me at all, did you? You only said the words, lied to me, to . . . to . . ."

"To get into your pants, sweetheart." Viciously, with contempt. "The only thing I ever cared about, baby, was that hot little fanny of yours. So there it is, all out in the open at last. Now are you going to get out of here, or would you like me to tell you some more? Like what a really lousy lay you are. And how I was thinking about other girls the whole time, even when I was—"

"No! Oh God, Larry, stop it! Stop it!"

"Then get out!"

Vague weeping sounds. Footsteps, rapid, retreating. Door slamming. Silence.

Now.

The limping man squatted and placed the shopping bag on the wet stone at his feet. He lifted out the gallon jug which had once contained apple cider, but which now contained the high-octane gasoline he had purchased at a Chevron station in Belmont forty-five minutes earlier. He removed the protective section of cellophane food wrap from the top and felt the strips of cotton sheeting which were stuffed into the bottle's neck. Dry. All right.

He got the windproof butane lighter from his overcoat pocket and straightened up, bringing the gallon jug with him, crooked in his left arm, and he held the lighter poised in his right. He flipped the cap down and his gloved thumb rasped the flint wheel. A thin, high jet of flame shot up. He held it to the sheet strips, watching them flare and begin to burn brightly, and then he stepped out to stand directly in front of the glassed archway, the jug held chest-high like a basketball about to be passed, and Green was there, with his back to him, ten feet away and moving, and almost casually then, the limping man thrust forward, releasing and stepping back, and the flaming container shattered the archway glass and shattered the stillness and shattered itself on the floor inside in a great, rushing, mushrooming sweep of heat and fire and destruction . . .

The sound of the archway glass breaking sends Larry Drexel whirling about, his eyes bulging wide in surprise and sudden fear, and there is in that moment an intense, bursting, undulating vortex of flame that sends him stumbling backward, trying to get his arm up to protect his eyes, but it is too late for that, too late, and the heat singes away his eyebrows and his eyelashes and blisters the skin of his face like a strip of paint under a blowtorch.

He goes to his knees with a scream erupting from his throat, high and shrill and containing every decibel of mortal terror. The flames spread with insane rapidity, licking at the walls, the furniture, the rug and the floor, consuming the scrolled desk, consuming the religious mural and the blue velvet nude, crackling, thundering, brilliant red-orange billowing smoke, searing heat. Drexel tries to stand, and the flames reach out for him, catch him, hold him, set his sleek black hair ablaze, and his shirt and jacket and trousers ablaze, and in the pain-thing that is his brain:

Oh God the heat the heat the heat I'm on fire I'm on fire help me Jesus Christ help me I'm on fire

He screams again, and again, and again, he can't stop screaming, and then he is on his feet and running, running toward the hallway and into it, running for the door, getting it open somehow, trailing fire, running outside, running blind, seeing nothing, feeling nothing but the heat and the pain, a human torch, screaming, dying . . .

The first thing Steve Kilduff saw was the orange glow flickering through the windows of the house.

He had just turned onto the Five-Hundred block of San Amaron Drive, and when he perceived the glow at two hundred yards he knew that the house was on fire. Intuitively, he sensed that it was Drexel's house, that it was Number 547, even though he was still too far away to read the number and to determine accurately the make and color of the sports car parked in the drive. His foot came off the accelerator and touched the brake, and the long conical beams of his headlights picked up the outline of a car parked in front of the house and picked up, too, the figure of a girl in a plastic raincoat standing immobile on the sidewalk, looking back.

And that was when the front door burst open and the man on fire came hurtling out.

Kilduff thought: My God, my God, my God! He knew that it was Drexel, knew with that same intuitive certainty that it was Drexel and that Helgerman had been responsible, had gotten to Number Five. He saw the burning man, Drexel, veer to the left, stumbling over the landscaped front yard, through bottle brush and barrel cactus and Joshua trees, across the drive at the rear of the sports car—and his foot came crashing down hard on the brake. The machine slewed violently sideways, the rear end coming around on the rain-slick macadam street, the front wheels skipping up over the low curb. Kilduff was out of the car before it had rocked to a full stop, out and running after Drexel, no indecision, no weighing and considering, he wasn't thinking at all; he was reacting, reflex, instinct, military training, pulling off his overcoat as he ran along the sidewalk, past the girl in the plastic raincoat. She was screaming, hysterical; and fifty yards away, bulling through a low thin hedge, Drexel was screaming with a different kind of hysteria. The night was alive with vibrating nightmare sounds.

Kilduff had the overcoat off now, and he closed the gap between himself and Drexel to twenty yards . . . fifteen . . . ten. They were on a wide expanse of neighboring lawn, on a cushiony surface dotted with rain ponds that glistened dancing silver highlights in the scintillation from the fanning, clinging flames. Kilduff overtook Drexel and threw the overcoat around him, the screams piercing his skin like long sharp needles, and pulled him down onto the wet grass. He held the overcoat around him, trying to smother the flames, his hands locked together at Drexel's belt, feeling the heat scorch his body through the heavy cloth. And then they were rolling over and over through the cold, wet grass and Kilduff was able to gain his knees beside Drexel, smelling the stench of burned hair and burned flesh, and vomit came up into his throat and gagged him. He pulled the overcoat back, and the flames had given way to rising puffs of blackly acrid smoke; but Kilduff kept rolling him back and forth on the puddled grass for a long, long time.

When he finally stopped, he could hear screaming again, from close behind him, and he knew it was the girl in the raincoat. He shut his eyes and opened them again and looked down at the charred, smoking body, looked down at it long enough to confirm what he already knew—that the man was Larry Drexel—and then he turned away and let the vomit come boiling out of his throat.

Light flooded over him as he rose to wipe his mouth, and a frightened woman's voice said, "I've called the police and the fire department—is that Mr. Drexel, is he dead?—oh dear Lord, I saw him running on fire . . ."

"Shut off that light," Kilduff said. "Shut it the hell off."

The light went off, and there was the sound of a door slamming. Kilduff got his arm under Drexel's head and lifted it up; with his other hand he found one of the wrists, still hot, and probed for a pulsebeat. He couldn't find one, and he thought that Drexel was dead; but then he realized the two terrible black-white things which had once been eyes were staring at him and somehow seeing him, somehow recognizing him, and the black gashed thing which had once been a mouth was working around a protruding tongue. Dry, brittle sounds came out, the sounds of twigs snapping in the darkness of a forest, and after that there were words, unrecognizable at first, but Kilduff put his ear very close to Drexel's mouth and he could understand some of them.

"Helgerman . . . listen . . . Helgerman . . ."

Kilduff wanted to vomit again. He wanted the girl behind him to stop screaming. He wanted to turn and run, get away from there, far, far away. But he said, "Don't try to talk, Larry," in a voice that was strangely gentle, strangely calm. "Don't try to talk."

But Drexel's mouth continued to work, and the brittle sounds that became words reached Kilduff's ears again. "Helgerman . . . dead . . . long-time dead."

And the brittle sounds ceased, and there was a single, barely audible, undeniably final exhalation of breath, and the blackened lump of flesh which had been Larry Drexel died shuddering in Kilduff's arms.

Orange Thursday

14

Thursday morning, 3:45 A.M.

Twin Peaks lay quiet and empty under an enveloping shroud of high, drifting fog and thinly cold rain-mist. The steep, winding expanse of Caveat Way was very dark, with only a single, pale-aureoled street lamp burning a half block from where the seemingly empty Ford Mustang was parked between two other cars.

But in the shadowed driver's seat, slumped down beneath the wheel until his eyes were on a level with the sill of the closed window, the limping man sat nervously waiting. On the seat beside him lay the American Tourister briefcase, the catches unfastened, the .44 Ruger Magnum resting just inside the joined halves. His eyes were watchful, probing now and then the silhouetted darkness which blanketed the glass entranceway to Orange's apartment building diagonally across the street.

He remained absolutely motionless, save for a soft, quick, nervous drumming of his fingers on the steering wheel. As he waited, he let his mind drift briefly to the recent events in Los Gatos.

He hadn't seen the actual immolation of Green, but the sweeping wall of fire flashing toward him had been enough; Green had not survived the holocaust. As for his own escape, he had accomplished that without incident. It had taken him only a matter of seconds to clear the stone-and-mortar wall at the rear of the patio and to make his way quickly down the bank to the creek bed. No one had seen him, he was certain of that. The dead-end street had still been as dark and deserted as when he had left it, and the cross-street was likewise void of traffic when he took the rented Mustang onto it moments later. He had debated driving around to San Amaron Drive to see first-hand what had happened, but had decided against that almost immediately; there was no use inviting unnecessary risk.

So it had all gone very nicely.

Now there was only the problem of Orange.

As he had driven back toward San Francisco, the limping man had considered his original plan. He did not care for the fact that Orange lived in an apartment in a well-populated area; not at all like Green, who lived in a residential neighborhood that afforded such safety factors as the swallowing darkness of the creek bed and the walled-in patio and the dead-end street. Reaching Orange in the sanctity of his apartment building, in the limiting surroundings of San Francisco itself, would be difficult—perhaps even foolhardy.

But Orange had to die—tonight, no later than dawn if at all possible.

He had considered the choices, the potentialities, and that fact was irrefutable. The proximity of Orange to Yellow and Green demanded the urgency, for there was no way of knowing if Orange knew of Yellow's death—he wouldn't know of Green's as yet—or of the deaths of Blue and Red and Gray. There was no way of determining if Orange suspected strongly or even mildly that he, too, was a target. The idea would certainly have occurred to him if he *was* aware of the facts. And if he did suspect anything amiss, there was no way, either, of determining what he would do when he learned of Green's death.

Would he run?

Would he hide, arm himself, wait it out?

Would he go to the police?

If he ran, or if he hid, he could be found again; but that would take time. It would take time, too, if Orange tried to wait him out—something that couldn't be accomplished. If Orange went to the police, it was possible that things would be much worse; it wasn't likely that that would be the case because Orange couldn't be certain of what was happening, even though he might suspect, and because of his complicity in the robbery eleven years ago. It would be a last resort, a panic move, but you couldn't get inside a man's mind to find out his breaking point. And if Orange did go to the police, and a thorough investigation was instigated, there was the possibility of discovery, always that possibility.

Another thing which had been a strong influence on the limping man's decision was the factor of time. He was tired of waiting—he had waited long enough, much too long—and there was only one man left now, one out of six. He wanted it to end, wanted it to be done now, finished, over with.

So to protect himself, and to appease himself, he had to kill Orange tonight—even if it meant using the Magnum instead of more fitting and ingenious ways, instead of striking swiftly, silently, blindly as he had with the others—at all costs.

The limping man had driven into San Francisco and up to Twin Peaks and into the Texaco station on the corner of Portola and Burnett. He had dropped a coin into the slot on the pay telephone there, and dialed Orange's number, waiting, intending to hang up when the connection was made, when he was certain Orange was home.

Only, the connection had not been made.

And when he had then driven to Caveat Way and looked into the open garage stall designated to Orange, he had found it empty. Orange was not home.

He hadn't liked that, not at all; it necessitated more waiting. But there was simply nothing he could do about it. Orange was out somewhere, no telling where, and he had no other choice but to wait for him to come home. He had parked the rented Mustang across the street, in a spot which afforded him a clear view of the darkened entranceway and the garage stall; and he had settled down to wait.

He had been waiting, now, for something over three hours. In that time he had seen no one enter the apartment building, had seen no one come out. There had been a few automobiles earlier, but none in the past half hour.

The limping man's fingers went on beating an impatient tattoo on the steering wheel. Abruptly, he ceased the steady rhythm to raise his wrist close to his eyes, shading the luminous dial of his watch with his other hand cupped around it: 4:02. Fingers again on the wheel, more agitated now. Goddamn it to hell, where was he? He should have been home by now, long ago . . .

Headlights loomed suddenly on the street, and the limping man tensed, drifting lower on the seat. He moved his hand inside the open briefcase to touch the cold, textured butt of the Magnum. But the car passed, moving swiftly, turning the corner left; it was a fifteen-year-old Buick with four darkly shadowed shapes inside, two in front and two in back. He relaxed somewhat, sliding his hand out of the case, drumming again.

Hell yes, Orange should have been home by this time. Then why *wasn't* he? Where had he gone? What was he doing at four in the morning? What time would he be back? Enough questions, too many questions, and none of them had any answers.

Unless . . .

Unless he wasn't *coming* home.

Unless he had already begun to run.

Or hide.

Unless he had already gone to the police.

The limping man wrapped his hands tightly around the slender circumference of the steering wheel, squeezing, squeezing. That could be it, all right, he thought, that could damned well be it. But which one? The police? No, he couldn't know of Green's death yet, and it would surely take that knowledge to send him to the authorities; no, it wasn't the police, he was sure enough of that to discard it. Running, then? Maybe. Where? Anywhere. Planes left San Francisco twenty-four hours a day, for all parts of the world . . . Damn, damn, I should have checked on him yesterday, but it's too late to worry about that now if he's on the wing, and he could be, he just could be. Or he could be hiding. Where? Anywhere. Hotels, motels, in the city and out of it . . .

Oh, wait now.

Yes! Yes!

There was one place Orange might go, one specific place, a place he would consider safe, a place he would feel certain no one outside his close circle of friends would know about—and surely not an unseen nemesis, underrating as he would the thoroughness, the tenacity of that enemy. A place he might go if he was no more than mildly suspicious, mildly worried, wanted only to take time to think things out; a place he might go even if he suspected nothing, wanted merely to escape the crush of a large city.

A logical place, under any circumstances.

A place called Duckblind Slough.

The limping man smiled grimly in the darkness. Should he wait any longer here? Decision: No. The more he thought of it, the more convinced he became that Orange might have gone, for one reason or another, to his small fishing cabin in Duckblind Slough, Petaluma River, Marin County. It would take him less than an hour to drive up there and find out, and if he was right, he could be on his way home sometime later this afternoon; peace at last, and perhaps a whore like Alice to share it with for a few hours. If he was wrong, he would call Orange's number again; had he returned home by then, somehow, there would still be enough time before dawn to accomplish his mission. And if Orange was not at the cabin, and had not returned home . . . well, there was no use in looking at the darker prospects now. He could cross such a bridge if and when he came to it.

The limping man straightened on the seat, his hand flicking out to turn the key in the ignition and bring the quiet engine to life, to switch on the lights, the windshield wipers, the heater-defroster. Moments later, he took the car out onto the slick, deserted street. There was almost no traffic, but he drove with a certain degree of caution; the last thing he needed at this moment was a confrontation with a police traffic patrol.

When he reached the Golden Gate Bridge, however, he drove more rapidly; less than a half hour later, he made the turn off Highway 101 onto the narrow dirt road leading toward the Petaluma River. It was raining harder here, and the wind was north and very strong, causing the bordering trees to bow, as he drove beneath them, like subjects fawning at the passage of a royal carriage. He passed the Mira Monte Marina and Boat Launch and the trap-shooting club, the private-property sign; he drove along the first private road until he reached the entrance to the second. Slowing as he made the turn, he switched off his headlights; when he had crossed the raised bank of the railroad spur tracks, he brought the Mustang to a silent stop at the padlocked wooden gate which barred the road at that point.

The limping man sat there for a moment, reconnoitering. Then he took the Ruger .44 Magnum from the briefcase on the seat beside him and put it into the pocket of his overcoat. He took the black pigskin gloves from the glove compartment, slipped them on, and stepped out into the wind and the rain.

He went directly to the gate, climbed it quickly and nimbly, the gloves protecting his hands from the sharp, rusted barbed wire strung across its top. He dropped down on the other side, pausing to rest his game leg, letting his eyes probe the black morass ahead. He could not see the shack from where he stood—it was better than a half-mile from the gate—but if there had been a light burning inside, he would have been able to discern it; the terrain was relatively flat, with no tall trees or shrubs to blot out any light. As it was, there was only darkness, full and absolute.

He put his right hand on the Ruger in his pocket and moved forward, walking swiftly along the muddied road, oblivious to the slanting rain which matted his thin hair to his scalp and ran in tiny tear-streams down along his face, oblivious to the pull of the icy, moaning wind.

It took him fifteen minutes to reach the circumscribed clearing which served as a parking area for the three fishing cabins in the slough. He saw the small, convex shape of a single automobile, standing like a wet and silent sentinel on the grassy, pooled clearing, and he thought: Volkswagen; Orange's wife has a Volkswagen.

He approached the car quietly, sliding his canvas shoes—soaked through now—along the slippery, mired ground. At the rear bumper he squatted and peered at the license plate. Yes, it belonged to the woman; he knew the number.

The limping man straightened, wiping water from his face with his gloved left hand. Was Orange here? Had he used his wife's car? But if so, why? Where was *his* car, the Pontiac? Had the two of them come up together? Were they both now inside the cabin? Or, for some reason, had his wife come here alone?

Well, there was only one way to find out.

He located the vegetation-entangled path leading to the point and began to make his way stealthily along it, his right hand still touching the Ruger Magnum in his overcoat pocket.

Andrea Kilduff sat bolt upright on the Army cot, clutching the heavy wool blankets tightly in both hands, her eyes suddenly opened wide like a frightened owl's in the darkness.

There had been a sound—unidentifiable, yet distinctly loud—and it had come from just outside the bedroom window . . .

She sat there, trembling a little, listening. The rain pounded, pounded on the roof of the shack as if demanding entrance, and there was the steady whistling bay of the wind. But there was nothing else now, no other sounds. Andrea swept the blankets back impulsively and padded barefoot to the window, staring out at the gray-black water of the slough and beyond it at the indistinguishable shapes and shadows of the marshland. Nothing moved save for the grasses and the tall rushes under the elemental onslaught.

Andrea looked at her watch, squinting in the blackness. It was 5:11. She shivered and went back to the cot and lay down and pulled the blankets up under her chin. My imagination, she thought; now I'm creating prowlers in the middle of nowhere. Well, it serves me right, I suppose. I simply shouldn't have come back here last night. I should have gone to Mona's, in El Cerrito, or at least back into San Francisco to a motel; it wasn't raining *that* hard and the traffic wasn't *that* heavy on the freeway. I must be going a little dotty to have wanted to spend another night in this place.

She wrapped the blankets even more tightly around herself, mummifying her body against the shack's chill. She closed her eyes and tried to regain the fragments of sleep—fitful and restless though it had been. But her mind was clear now, clear and alert; it wasn't any use.

She lay there and wished Steve had been home last night, she wished she'd been able to talk to him and get it all said then and there; but now, at least, she knew from talking to Mrs. Yarborough that he hadn't moved out, and there was always today. She would call him this morning; he was sure to be home this morning. Of course, she could drive to San Francisco and see him face to face, she could do that, but it was really out of the question. It was going to be difficult enough to say the words as it was, and if necessary, they could see one another at some later date—well no, now no, it was probably better if they just didn't see one another at all, ever again.

Andrea closed her eyes and pictured Steve's face in her mind, his face as it looked sleeping or in complete repose, like a child's, like a very small and very handsome and very mischievous little boy. She felt little quivering sensations in her stomach, and opened her eyes again, and sighed, and thought: I don't want to see him again, I really don't, I have to adjust and that isn't easy and won't be easy and seeing him will only make matters worse, more difficult, so it's better if I just call him today and get it all said and then I can go . . .

Where?

Where will I go?

She shivered again. I have to go somewhere, she thought, I have to start over again somewhere. Oakland? Could I still get a job with Prudential Life? It's been seven years since I've worked at anything except being a wife, but you never really forget any skills, that's what they say, and secretarial work is a skill, so I shouldn't have forgotten how to do it. But do I want to live in Oakland, in the Bay Area, close to Steve, knowing he's nearby? No—but where else would I go? I don't *know* where to go when I leave here, big cities like New York and Chicago frighten me, a little town then, a little town somewhere, but I don't think I'd like that either. Where will I go? I have to go somewhere. Mona and Dave? Well, maybe that's it; yes, Mona and I have always been close and they have a large enough house, they won't mind putting me up for a while, I can pay them room and board once I get a job, yes, that's where I'll go, at least for a while.

But she didn't feel any better. The implications and the immense loneliness of the question *Where will I go?* had left her feeling small and empty and unwanted, friendless and loveless, naked and alone in a vast, populated wilderness. Lying there in the darkness, she was afraid again. The sooner she called Steve, the sooner she could leave Duckblind Slough for good. After she talked to him, she could call Mona and tell her about it and then she could go over to El Cerrito and they'd have a long, maudlin cry together. What she needed now was companionship, someone to talk to; when you're alone for too long you start dwelling in the depths of gloom and depression, feeling sorry for yourself and looking at life through a glass darkly. Once she had a different perspective, things wouldn't seem quite so—

There was the sound of a footfall on the porch outside.

Andrea sat up again, and her heart began to hammer violently. Was somebody out there? No, that was impossible; who would be out there, in the rain, at five o'clock in the morning? No, it was just her imagination, that's all, just her—

The doorknob rattled.

Again.

Again.

Something smashed against the flimsy wood of the door.

Andrea threw the blankets back, stumbling off the cot to stand just inside the open doorway, hand held up to her mouth, her eyes bulging with consuming terror.

The door burst open.

It burst open, and a man stood framed in the doorway, framed in silhouette against the adumbral sky and the driving rain, a blackly faceless man with something held extended in one hand, something that gleamed dully in the pale, painted-rust glow from the fire in the stove.

Andrea began to scream.

15

He was the last one left.

Steve Kilduff, man alone.

He sat in the kitchen of the Twin Peaks apartment, and stared into the cup of black coffee. It was past dawn now, Thursday morning, and he could see, through the partially draped window-doors the length of the apartment, the gray sky with its dotting of gray-black clouds—tainted chunks of butter floating in tainted buttermilk.

And, as if superimposed on the bleak patina of the newborn day:

Larry Drexel, lying on the cold wet grass—blackened and foully reeking and dead . . .

Himself, kneeling beside the charred body, now standing, now backing away . . .

The girl in the plastic raincoat, taking his place on the grass, burying her face in her hands . . .

Faces—featureless, oddly disembodied—watching the flames and staring at the dead man; pagan worshippers at the shrine of horror . . .

His car, ignition, brake, reverse, drive forward—going where?—going nowhere . . .

Police cars with flashing red dome-lights, and fire engines with high brightly yellow-white eyes . . .

Freeway lights, the same surrealistic montage of red and yellow, red and yellow, rushing forward, going nowhere as he was going nowhere, until fear sent him panicked onto an exit ramp to seek escape . . .

Interior shot: a cocktail lounge, locationless, nameless, dark, almost deserted, and the glass in his hand, trembling, full, and the glass in his hand, trembling, empty . . .

Dark, rain-swept, maze-like streets and roads and county highways, empty and strange, leading somewhere, yet leading nowhere, turn left, turn right, turn around . . .

Freeway again, an incalculable time later, the motion slower now, not so frightening, fewer yellows and fewer reds, and the rain had abated somewhat . . .

The dead, lonely streets of San Francisco under the first pale filtered light that signified the coming of dawn, daybreak of the morning after the final holocaust, and he was the lone survivor, the last man on earth, coming home . . .

He could see all of that vividly, but it was all in his mind, and in his mind, too, were the sounds, nightmare sounds of screaming and wailing sirens and driving rain and hurtling machines, and above it all were Larry Drexel's brittle, dying, whispered words:

"Helgerman . . . dead . . . long-time dead."

He had been sitting there at the dinette for—how long? two hours? three?—sitting there and staring into the cold coffee, trying to keep from losing his grip on reality, from blowing his mind finally and irrevocably, feeling the awful pressure slowly but inexorably begin to lessen until, now, he knew a kind of unstable calm. He could look at the mental images, and hear the mental sounds, and there was no panic. He could be objective now, he could examine what had happened and determine its effect, he could be rational.

Helgerman is dead, he thought, it isn't Helgerman; Drexel said it isn't Helgerman and he was dying when he said it and there can be no disputation of the words of a dying man. So it isn't Helgerman, Helgerman is dead, it isn't Helgerman of the injured neck, Helgerman the wronged, Helgerman who had been struck down in the parking lot, Helgerman the only man it *could* be; it isn't Helgerman. Then—who is it? Who pushed Jim Conradin off that cliff, and who set fire to Larry Drexel, and who murdered Cavalacci and Wykopf and Beauchamp? Who was waiting for him, Steve Kilduff, out there somewhere in the cold gray morning and in the dark black night? Who wanted him dead, as he had wanted and had made the others dead? What was the reason, the rationale, in a mind surely twisted?

Who?

And why?

But even more urgently important, what am I going to do now? Do I somehow seek out and somehow kill this now-nameless, now-faceless, non-existent but all-so-terribly-real madman—as Drexel would have done? Do I avenge the deaths of the others, and in so doing save my own life? Or do I go to the police, as I should have done in the very beginning? Or do I curl up in a tiny ball like a naked hedgehog and wait defenseless for whoever it is to come for me? Or do I run out of the state, out of the country, always looking over my shoulder, always trembling, always running?

What do I do?

The only thing I can do.

I'm not a killer, I never will be a killer, I could never find the man alone, and I would be as mad as he must be to believe I can. And I don't want to die any more than any man wants to die; and the only place I could run—my eventual destination next week or next month or next year—would be off the deep end, right off the deep end. I have one alternative left, then. I go to the police. I go to Inspector Commac and Inspector Flagg and I tell them all about it, I tell them the whole story and I ask them to protect me and they will protect me and they will find the madman, whoever he is; I simply go to the police, and it's over for me, it's finished, no more fear, no more terror, it's over.

But can I do it?

Can I go in there and pick up that telephone and dial that number and say the words that have to be said? Did what I saw and heard and smelled and was a part of last night—the horror of last night—somehow give me enough guts to do what I wasn't able to do yesterday? Have I regained something of myself, a part of my manhood, that which enables a man to do what he must do?

Or is cowardice, once ingrained, not so easily dispelled?

Like a terminal malignancy, does it only spread until it consumes and destroys the being? And like that same malignancy, does it bring brief moments like these now—moments of painless calm, of commanding will, of hope—only to banish them, and return even more relentlessly destructive than before?

Kilduff got to his feet, pushing his chair back, and walked very slowly toward the hallway telephone. To find out if he was still a man.

It was just eight o'clock when Inspector Neal Commac stepped out of the elevator on the fourth floor of San Francisco's Hall of Justice. He walked along the quiet hallway and through a doorway marked with the sign: GENERAL WORKS DETAIL. It was a huge room with pale plaster walls and a reception desk on his immediate right and several glass-fronted interrogation cubicles beyond an open archway. The detective bull pen contained several metal desks in no particular order, with typewriters on metal roll stands beside them.

Commac nodded a perfunctory good morning to the receptionist, turned to the right and then to the left to a doorway beyond, entering the bull pen. At the desk facing his, in the center of the room, Inspector Pat Flagg was just hanging up his telephone. Steam spiraled upward from a container of coffee at his elbow. He looked up as Commac took off his hat and sat down.

"Morning, Neal."

"Pat."

Flagg indicated a covered container identical to the one on his desk, resting on Commac's blotter. "Brought you some coffee."

"Thanks," Commac said gratefully. "I could use some. It's a bear out this morning."

"We're in for a hell of a winter."

"Yeah." Commac slipped the plastic cover off the container and tasted the coffee. He made a wry face and looked at Flagg over the rim of the container. "What's on tap?"

"So far, just a talk with Mr. Brokaw on that attempted extortion in Sea Cliff."

"Any special time?"

"After eleven."

"Okay."

"Oh, and the DMV report came back on that '59 Personnel Roster we got from the Bellevue Air Force Station."

"Anything?"

Flagg picked up a printed form from his blotter. "Six with registered automobiles in California," he said. "Conradin and Kilduff; Thomas Baird, North Hollywood; Lawrence Drexel, Los Gatos; Dale Emmerick, Redding; Victor Jobelli, Yreka."

"You run those last four through R&I?"

"What I was doing when you came in."

Commac nodded. "I wonder if we'll turn anything there."

"Is that a question, or are you thinking out loud?"

"A little of both, I guess."

Flagg said, "Probably draw the same blank we did on Kilduff and Conradin."

"Is that a considered opinion, or are you just being cynical?"

Flagg grinned. "A little of both, I guess."

The phone on Commac's desk buzzed; it was an interdepartmental call. He depressed the button and lifted the receiver. He listened for a moment, said "Yes, sir," and replaced the instrument. To Flagg he said, "Boccalou wants to see us, Pat."

"What on?"

"He didn't say."

"Well," Flagg said, getting to his feet, "here we go."

They went across the bull pen and Commac knocked on a door marked: CHIEF OF DETECTIVES. A voice said to come in. They stepped inside and stood respectfully before the desk of Chief Nello Boccalou. Boccalou had inscrutable green eyes, a firm chin with a Kirk Douglas cleft, and longish silver hair that gave him a leonine and properly authoritative appearance. He smoked imported English tobacco in a long-grain briar pipe, and the office was filled with gray-blue clouds of aromatic smoke. He said, "Commac, Flagg."

"Morning, Chief," Commac said.

"Turn anything new on this Kilduff you questioned yesterday?"

"Not yet, sir," Flagg told him.

Boccalou took the pipe out of his mouth and scowled at it and put it in an ashtray. "Well, I may have something for you. Squeal from the Los Gatos police."

"Oh?"

"Seems they had a fire-bombing down there last night. Local man killed, assailant or assailants unknown. There were a couple of witnesses—neighbors, the dead man's pregnant girlfriend, and an unidentified man who chased after the victim when he came running out of the burning house, clothes afire. This unidentified man managed to put the flames out, but it was too late; before the fire department and the Gatos officers arrived, he took off. The girlfriend was hysterical, but when they got her to a hospital and calmed down, she managed to give them a description of the unidentified and a partial on the license plate of his car. One of the neighbors supplied the rest of the plate, and Gatos ran it through DMV. Who do you suppose the car belongs to?"

"Steve Kilduff," Commac said immediately.

"Uh-huh," Boccalou said. "Description matches, too. Gatos has a want on him for questioning. They're requesting we pick him up."

"What's the name of the guy who died?" Flagg asked. "The Gatos resident?"

Boccalou looked at a form on his desk. "Drexel," he answered. "Lawrence Drexel."

Commac and Flagg exchanged glances. "He's on the Bellevue Personnel Roster," Commac said. "He was stationed with Kilduff and Conradin."

"It looks like a tie-in on the Smithfield unsolved, then."

"Yeah, it sure does."

"Go on over to this Kilduff's apartment and bring him in on a hold for Gatos," Boccalou said. "We'll see what he has to say for himself."

"Right."

While they were waiting for the elevator to take them down into the vehicle garage in the basement of the Hall of Justice, Commac said, "How does this whole thing look to you, Pat?"

"Like there's more to it than we might first credit," Flagg answered.

"I've been thinking the same thing."

"Any ideas?"

"Not really."

"Do you think Kilduff had something to do with this Drexel's death last night?"

"Boccalou said he was the one who tried to save him."

"Yeah."

Commac rubbed the back of his neck. "Kilduff was scared when we talked to him yesterday. Scared shitless. The way you're scared if somebody's got a gun to the back of your neck."

"I had that feeling, too," Flagg said. "But I can't figure an angle either. Hell, it's been eleven years since that Smithfield job. Why, all of a sudden, should the guys who pulled it off—if Kilduff and the others *are* the guys who pulled it off—begin dying mysteriously?"

"There's the obvious answer."

"One of their own, you mean?"

"Uh-huh."

"It doesn't add," Flagg said. "The time factor is all wrong. The only logical motive would be the money, and eleven years makes that ludicrous."

"Yeah, I know."

"So what else can it be?"

"That I *don't* know."

"Maybe Kilduff does."

"Well, if he doesn't," Commac said, "he's got a pretty good idea."

The elevator doors slid open and they stepped inside. They rode down to the basement in silence.

16

He had entered the hallway, walking stiffly, purposefully, and he was reaching out for the telephone receiver when the bell shrilled at him. He came up short, pulling his hand back as if the sudden cacophonous sound had somehow imparted a physical shock. He stood there listening to his heart plunge in his chest, and the bell rang a second time, and a third, and then he put out his hand and caught up the receiver and put it to his ear. He said "Hello?" carefully, guardedly.

"Mr. Kilduff?" an unfamiliar masculine voice said. "Mr. Steven Kilduff?"

"Yes," he said. "Yes, speaking."

"My name is Fazackerly, Deputy Sheriff Ed Fazackerly. I'm with the Marin County Sheriff's Office."

He frowned, working his tongue over his lips. Now what? he thought. Jesus, now what? He said, "I . . . don't understand."

"You own a small fishing cabin on the Petaluma River, is that correct? In Duckblind Slough?"

"Why . . . yes, that's right."

"Well, we're investigating the death by drowning of a young woman found about seven this morning near the dock at the rear of your cabin," Fazackerly said. "Two foul-weather fishermen trolling the slough for catfish saw her floating face down in the water there. They summoned us immediately."

A cold thing began to work its way slowly up along Kilduff's back. "I'm sorry," he said, "but I don't—"

"We subsequently found evidence of recent occupancy of your cabin, Mr. Kilduff."

"You mean somebody's been living there?"

"Yes, for the past few days. You weren't aware of this fact, I take it."

"No. No, I wasn't."

"I wonder if I might speak to your wife?"

"My wife?" he asked, and the cold thing grew colder.

"Yes. Is she at home now?"

"No, she's not here."

"May I ask where she is?"

"I . . . don't know."

"Would you mind explaining that?"

"We . . . we separated last week . . ." Pause—one heartbeat, two—and then the automatic and immediate defensive barriers constructed by his brain collapsed, and the inescapable implications of Fazackerly's words overwhelmed him. His knees seemed to buckle, as if the joints had somehow liquefied, and the cold thing froze his spine into humped rigidity, and a terrible tingling pain flashed upward through his groin, into his belly, into his chest, taking the breath away from him momentarily.

The telephone crackled. "Mr. Kilduff?"

The hard rubber circle of the receiver crushed his ear painfully against the side of his head. He fought air into his lungs, and they responded convulsively, expanding, contracting, and he got words out then, breaking a silence that was, in his ears, as loud as the combing of surf in a storm: "Jesus God, you don't think *Andrea* is—?"

"I'm sorry, Mr. Kilduff," Fazackerly said. "We found your wife's car, a tan Volkswagen, parked in the clearing in front, and her purse was inside the cabin, on the table. Your name was on her insurance ID card as next of kin . . ."

He stood there, motionless, and after a long moment thick, liquid, tremulous words came out of his throat: "How . . . how did it happen? God, how . . . ?"

"We have no way of being certain," Fazackerly said quietly. "It's been storming heavily up here for the past couple of days. There's the possibility that she was walking along the bank for some reason, and an undermined section gave way and toppled her into the slough. That water can be treacherous at this time of year, as you surely know. Was your wife a good swimmer?"

"She couldn't swim at all," he said numbly. "How—long has she . . . ?"

"It appears as if she was in the water about twelve hours, Mr. Kilduff."

"Twelve hours."

"I'm sorry to have to break such tragic news over the telephone," Fazackerly said. His voice was sympathetic. "But we're understaffed here and we couldn't send a man down personally. I hope you understand."

". . . yes . . ."

"We haven't moved the—remains as yet; we'd like a positive identification first. Will you be able to come to Duckblind Slough right away?"

"Yes, within an hour . . . within an hour . . ."

He broke the connection. He put his thumb on the button and held it down, the receiver still clasped tightly in his left hand. He was trembling now, and his face was flushed and sheened with tiny globules of sweat, and there was ice on his back and under his arms and between his legs.

Andrea was dead.

Andrea was dead!

He dropped the receiver suddenly and turned and ran into the kitchen. He stopped by the table, putting his hands flat on the Formica top. He looked wildly about him. The walls began to move—he could see them moving—pale white vertical planes reaching for him, going to crush him, and he choked off the scream that spiraled into his throat, and turned again and ran into the living room. He fumbled at the pull-catches on the sliding glass window-doors, breaking a fingernail, and then he had them open. He ran out onto the balcony and stood there with his palms braced against the slippery wet iron railing.

Andrea was dead.

He opened his mouth and sucked ravenously the cold wet air, his chest heaving as if it were a blacksmith's bellows. The shock of it entering his lungs eased the pressure that had been forming within his skull, and he straightened up, pivoting, looking back into the apartment. He felt the rain then, and the frigidity of the morning, and he stepped forward into the warmth of the living room again, shutting the window-doors behind him. Duckblind Slough, he thought, and he went on enervated legs into the bedroom and opened the paneled door on his half of the walk-in closet and took out his heavy wool topcoat. He laid it over his arm, walking back into the living room now, walking swiftly, and he went to the front door and threw it open.

The woman standing in the hallway outside said "Oh!" in a small, startled voice, and took a step backward.

Kilduff said, "Christ!" He tried to move around her.

But the woman had recovered now, and she came forward again, blocking him. She was tall and angular, middle-aged, with short, layered reddish-brown hair. She held her hands as if she wasn't quite sure what to do with them, elbows in close to her sides, palms turned upward, fingers spread and somewhat overlapping. She wore a multicolored silk muumuu and an old gray sweater around her shoulders.

He said, "Mrs. Yarborough, for God's sake!"

"I have to talk to you, Mr. Kilduff," she said rapidly, as if she wanted to get those words out—and the ones which were to follow—before she forgot them. "I really do, it won't take very long, now you *know,* Mr. Kilduff, that I'm not a woman to pry into the affairs of my neighbors but I really do like you and Andrea, she and I have become very close friends you know, of course when I didn't see her these past few days I thought perhaps she was visiting her sister, I had no idea you were *separated,* I really didn't, until . . ."

Not now, not now! Oh goddamn it, why did she have to come around *now?* He wanted to tell her to shut up, shut up, he wanted to tell her Andrea was dead: "Do you hear me, *Andrea—is—dead!*" But all he could say was her name, Mrs. Yarborough, and that was ineffective against the rushing, breathless flow of words.

". . . until she called me last night to ask if you had moved away because she'd tried to call you and you weren't home and she was naturally upset, of course I told her no you *hadn't* moved away, at least not that I knew about and you would surely tell me if you had since I'm the building manager, but you can't imagine how surprised I was to hear from the poor thing like that, oh she sounds so miserable, Mr. Kilduff, she really does, that's the reason I came up here this morning, now you understand I'm not a woman to pry into the affairs of my neighbors but I thought perhaps if you were to drive up to that fishing cabin of yours and just *talk* to her, I mean well she's been there for five days now, I feel so *sorry* for her, Mr. Kilduff, she sounded so helpless, after all it was the middle of the night and I didn't sleep at all not a wink after we hung up, thinking of her out driving alone in all this rain we've been having, alone up at that cabin—"

"What?" he said. "What did you say?"

She opened her mouth, and then closed it again. She looked at him blankly. He reached up and took hold of her shoulders, roughly, and his eyes bored into hers, making her cringe a little at the sudden fire which burned brightly there.

"What did you say?" he repeated. His voice was flat now, without inflection, and very soft.

"I . . . well, I don't know what you—"

"The middle of the night. You said Andrea called you in the middle of the night."

"Well, it wasn't really the middle of the night, I suppose, I go to bed early during the winter months because of—"

"What time did she call you!"

"It was . . . after eleven sometime," Mrs. Yarborough said hesitantly, a little frightened now. "I . . . I'm not sure what the exact time was, but it was after eleven . . ."

After eleven sometime. After eleven. He released her shoulders and stepped back, and his heart was hammering loudly, crazily, against his chest cavity. After eleven sometime.

It appears as if she was in the water about twelve hours, Mr. Kilduff . . .

Twelve hours. Found at seven this morning. Twelve hours. Time of death would have to have been around seven last night, but she had called Mrs. Yarborough after eleven. Eleven P.M. to seven A.M. Eight hours. Less than eight hours. And Fazackerly had said twelve hours, and a doctor or a coroner or a medical examiner or whoever the hell it was who examined a dead body couldn't make a mistake of four hours, could he? No, it was impossible, impossible.

Then—?

Fazackerly had been lying.

Sweet Mother of God, Fazackerly had been lying and the only reason he could have been lying was because he *wasn't* a deputy sheriff with the Marin County Sheriff's Office, wasn't even named Fazackerly; he was the killer, the nameless and faceless murderer of five men, setting up Number Six, the last one left. What better spot than Duckblind Slough—isolated, desolate—what more fitting spot? How he had known of the shack there wasn't important; he had known and he had gone there and Andrea had been there, Andrea had been there for the past five days . . .

But he had lied about the twelve hours.

Andrea had been alive, and safe, between eleven and midnight.

If she was dead, if he had killed her, why had he lied about the twelve hours? What reason would he have for lying about that?

No reason, none at all . . .

Abruptly, then, his legs moved, carrying him forward, past Mrs. Yarborough, almost knocking her down. He hit the stairs running.

Because maybe, just maybe, dear God, just maybe Andrea was still alive!

She lay huddled foetus-like, cold and afraid on the floor of the storage closet, lay in the Stygian blackness and listened to the vague, muted sounds of wind and rain, and to the imagined gnawings of a dozen rats in the mud beneath the shack's rough wood flooring. The nylon fishing line which bound her hands and her ankles was mercilessly taut, and her splayed fingers were numb against the cross-grained boards of the rear wall behind her. The strip of cloth which had been tied tightly, painfully, across her mouth tasted of grease, of must, of darkly crawling microbes.

She had been in there less than an hour.

She had harbored the idea, at first, of trying to kick down the closet door—the wood was old and very dry, and the hasp was somewhat rusted—and then crawling into the other room and finding a sharp knife or breaking a glass and using one of the shards to cut the nylon line. But the closet space was cramped, allowing no room for maneuverability, for leverage; if she had been a man, with a man's strength and stamina, with a man's bravery, she might still have been able to do it. But she wasn't, she was a small frightened woman, and she could only lie there, shivering in the darkness, waiting, waiting for him to come back, waiting for the nondescript, innocuous-looking man who walked with a noticeable limp.

And who had the eyes of a madman.

Andrea began to tremble again as she thought about those eyes. They were wide, penetrating, soulless; they looked through you, burned holes in you; they contained something indefinably but unmistakably terrifying. She had almost fainted the first time she'd seen them in the illumination from the Coleman pressure lantern, seen how the black, black pupils reflected the light and gave the impression of flames dancing and flickering deep within their inner recesses.

In that moment, she had fully expected him to kill her.

After performing unspeakable atrocities on her flesh.

But he hadn't touched her, except to slap her once very hard with the palm of his left hand when he had broken in, commanding her as he did so to stop screaming. When she had complied, he had told her in a flat, toneless voice that nothing would happen to her if she was quiet and responsive—not elaborating what he meant by responsive—and that was when he had put on the Coleman lantern and she had seen his eyes. She had had to exercise a tremendous effort of will to keep from panicking at that moment, to keep from screaming again, but she had done so, sitting on the Army cot and pulling the wool blanket up to cover her body even though she was clad in heavy lemon-colored pajamas. He had only nodded, and then had dragged in one of the chairs from the half-table and sat down on it facing her, crossing his legs and holding the gun very loosely, very casually on his knee, watching her, not speaking for a long while.

Who was he, who was he? The question had echoed and re-echoed in Andrea's mind as she sat before him, not looking at his eyes. Was he a madman, an escaped mental patient from some institution? She had tried to remember if there were any hospitals for mentally unbalanced people, any asylums, in the vicinity; but she didn't think there were, it wasn't likely. Was he an itinerant, a tramp? She had heard stories about hobos and drifters riding the northbound freights that rolled frequently by on the spur tracks a half-mile distant, about how they sometimes jumped off in isolated areas such as this one and went looking for food and shelter and money and . . . other things. But this man was too well-dressed, too well-groomed, too calm and systematic to be a tramp, to have been riding in a freight car. But who *was* he, then? Who else could he be? What did he want? What was he going to do?

He had said suddenly, "Where's your husband, Mrs. Kilduff?"

It had surprised her. It had surprised her enough so that she hadn't immediately been able to reply. He had asked the question again, with menace, with impatience, and she'd managed at length, "I . . . don't know where he is. Why? Why do you want to know where he is?"

"He isn't staying here with you?"

"No."

"Then why are you here?"

She hadn't been able to lie to him, hadn't been able to hedge an answer. It was his eyes, those omniscient eyes. "Because I . . . I've left him."

No visible reaction. "How long have you been here?"

"Since . . . last Saturday."

"Does Orange know you're here?"

". . . Orange?"

"Your husband."

"No, no . . . I don't think so."

"When was the last time you spoke to him?"

"Last Friday," Andrea said. "Please, what do you want with Steve? Do you know him?"

"I know him," the limping man had answered, and that had been all he'd said, lapsing into silence then, a silence which she hadn't been capable of breaking even though her mind was seething with new questions, new fears.

He had called Steve "Orange"; she'd heard him clearly. What did that mean? Was it some kind of nickname? Did he have Steve mixed up with someone else? No, that wasn't it; he had called her "Mrs. Kilduff" and he had come here to Duckblind Slough. He must have known Steve rather well—not many people were aware of the existence of this shack. But why had he thought Steve would be here now, in November? And how could her husband know a man like this, a man with insane eyes, a man who carried a gun? And what possible reason could this man have for wanting to locate him? To . . . dear Lord, to *kill* him? That would explain why he had the gun, but . . . no, that was crazy, why would anyone want Steve dead? It was a nightmare, this whole thing was a nightmare . . .

Time had passed, crawling. She had lost control momentarily, with the questions and the fears commingling in her brain, and had begun to cry. She'd sat on the cot, rocking to and fro, and the tears had fallen, cascading from her eyes. The limping man had said nothing, watching her, until there were no more tears and she was silent again. He'd seemed to be deeply immersed in thought, in some private and hideous contemplation.

Dawn had come, finally, diminishing the long shadows within the shack slowly, consuming the darkness until Andrea had been able to see through the window that the sky was once again wet gray gossamer. What was he waiting for? she had thought then. If he was going to kill her, rape her, why didn't he have done with it? Was he trying to torture her by making her wait, wait in silence, by giving her all this time to think about what would happen to her? It was inhuman—

Abruptly, as if he had reached some decision or formulated some plan, the limping man had gotten to his feet. He had held the gun pointed at her, moving to the storage closet, opening the door, peering alternately at what lay on the shelves inside and at Andrea sitting on the cot. He had taken the nylon fishing line down finally—new line wound carefully about a small wooden stake—and had instructed her to lie on her stomach across the cot with her hands clasped behind her. She had obeyed, sobbing again, tasting the fear in her mouth and in her throat, feeling it surge in her stomach.

He had put the gun into the pocket of his overcoat and methodically bound her hands and ankles. When he had finished, he'd picked her up, not straining under her weight at all, and carried her to the closet and placed her on the floor inside, where she now lay. His breath on her face had been fetid, though now she knew that fear and imagination had only made it seem that way.

Moments later she'd heard him leave the shack.

Her fear, now, was almost evenly divided. She feared for her own welfare; there was the uncertainty of whether or not he would come back—and if he did, what he would do to her. And she feared for Steve's welfare; she knew that he was in danger, terrible danger, that something of which she knew nothing, something of great magnitude, was terribly, terribly wrong.

But she could only lie there as she had done for the past hour, lie there cold and frightened and in the darkness and listen to the rain and wind, to the imagined gnawings of a dozen rats in the sucking mud beneath the closet floor.

Lie there and wait.

Just wait.

For—what?

Oh God, *for what?*

17

Inspectors Neal Commac and Pat Flagg arrived at the Caveat Way, Twin Peaks, address of Steven Kilduff a few minutes past eight-thirty. Flagg parked the plain black departmental sedan directly opposite the building, and they hurried across the rain-flooded width of the street and through the single glass-and-wood door in the glassed entranceway.

Commac took off his hat and brushed the beaded droplets of water from the crown. He said, "I wish this goddamned rain would let up. It puts me in a mood."

"Yeah," Flagg said. "I know."

They climbed the inside stairs and walked down the hallway and stopped before the door to Kilduff's apartment. Commac put his right forefinger on the ivory button of the doorbell, opening his suit coat with his left hand and pushing the tail back over the service revolver at his side belt. Flagg did the same. They had talked about it driving over in the sedan, and even though they didn't anticipate any trouble, they were being occupationally cautious.

They waited in the quiet hallway. There was no response, and no sound from within the apartment. They looked at one another, and then Commac shrugged lightly and depressed the bell button again.

Nothing.

Flagg said, "He's not home."

"Looks that way."

"Do you think he's flown?"

"Maybe," Commac said. "Let's see if the building manager knows where he is."

They walked downstairs again and looked at the redwood-framed bank of mailboxes set into the stucco-and-mica wall of the vestibule. Then they went back up one flight and knocked on the door of Apartment 204.

After a moment, a tall, handsome woman with reddish-brown hair opened the door and looked out at them quizzically. "Yes?" she said. "May I help you?"

"You're Mrs. Yarborough, the manager?" Commac asked.

"Yes, that's right."

"We're police officers," he said. "We'd like to ask you a couple of questions about one of the apartment holders."

She blinked at the badge pinned to the inside of the leather case in Commac's hand. Then she said "Which one?" a little breathlessly.

"Steven Kilduff."

"I knew it!" Mrs. Yarborough said. Her eyes were brightly sparkling. "I just knew it, the way he ran out of here a little while ago, acting so peculiarly, it just had to be something else beside the fact that Andrea was—"

Commac said, "Andrea? That would be Mr. Kilduff's wife, is that right?"

"Yes, well she's his wife *now* but she left him, you know, last Saturday although I didn't find out about it until last night when she called me, but just the mere fact that Andrea was spending a few days at their fishing cabin, poor thing, to think things over wasn't why he was acting so peculiarly, of course I don't exactly know what it was but since you're here I imagine it must be something very important?" She stopped, looking at them expectantly.

Commac touched the lobe of his right ear. "You said something about a fishing cabin, Mrs. Yarborough. Is that where Mr. Kilduff went, to the best of your knowledge?"

"Well, I suppose it is," Mrs. Yarborough said. "Of course, he didn't say, you understand he was acting so peculiarly and I make it a practice never to pry into the affairs of my neighbors but I just had to tell him about Andrea, poor thing, all alone and simply pining away for him, now you understand she's not involved in this police business, whatever it is, I can vouch for her character she's such a sweet girl, but if you could just tell me what it is Mr. Kilduff has done perhaps I—"

"Would you happen to know where this fishing cabin is, ma'am?" Flagg asked patiently.

"Well, not exactly, it's in Marin County somewhere, on that little river that runs into San Pablo Bay—"

"Petaluma River?" Commac asked.

"Yes, I think so, but now—"

"You don't know the exact location of the cabin?"

"In some slough or other, I think, Andrea mentioned it but I can't seem to recall, now really, Officers, don't you think I'm entitled to know why you want to talk to Mr. Kilduff, I've been cooperative, haven't I? and I think as the manager of the building that I'm—"

"What exactly did Mr. Kilduff say to you prior to his leaving, ma'am?" Flagg asked.

"What did he say?" Mrs. Yarborough put her hands on her hips and looked at them in an exasperated way. "Well, I was telling him about Andrea and all of a sudden he grabbed me by the shoulders, very roughly, and he demanded to know what time she had called and I told him it was after eleven sometime, and that was when he got this very peculiar look in his eyes and ran out of here, now if you don't mind, Officers, I'd like to know just what it is—"

"Thank you, Mrs. Yarborough," Commac said quietly. "We appreciate your assistance."

He nodded to Flagg and they turned and started for the stairs. Just as they reached the landing, there was the sound of a door slamming, very loudly, behind them. As they started down, Flagg said, "What do you make of it?"

"I'm not sure," Commac said.

"Do we follow it up?"

"I think we'd better."

"So do I."

"I don't see why Boccalou won't give us the okay, as long as the duty roster's clear enough," Commac said. "There's something more to this whole thing than just an eleven-year-old armored-car robbery, we both agree to that. I think he sees it that way, too."

Flagg nodded.

"We'll have to have the Marin County Sheriff's Department run a check on property owners, to find out where this fishing cabin of Kilduff's is located. They could have the information for us by the time we pulled into San Rafael to pick up one of their boys."

They reached the vestibule. "It's still raining, for Christ's sake," Commac said rhetorically, a little sourly, and they went out and ran across the street to the unmarked departmental sedan.

I still love her, Steve Kilduff thought.

I never stopped loving her at all.

He had just come down off Waldo Grade, and was approaching Richardson's Bay Bridge. Traffic was relatively light northbound, although the always-heavy southbound commuter traffic was predictably snarled by the rain and the attendant poor visibility. He was driving very fast for conditions, upwards of seventy-five, passing cars and changing lanes automatically, praying with a small part of him that he wouldn't encounter a Highway Patrolman, praying with the rest of him that Andrea was still alive. That was when he realized consciously what he had felt and known deep within him all along—that Andrea was an integral, inseparable part of his mind and of his soul; that a portion of his being had died when he believed she had died, and been reborn with the fervent chance that she was still alive, and would die again if this were not to be so; that he loved her as much now as he had that first day in Sugar Pine Valley.

And he knew other things then, just as certainly.

He knew that Andrea had not left him because of the money, that it had been, instead, because of Steve Kilduff—his weaknesses, the long endless string of failures. He had leaned on her, fed on her like a parasite, and she had dutifully carried him, loving him, never complaining, carried the weight of him on her shoulders all these years, the incredible weight of him, and finally the weight had simply become unbearable; what else could she do then *but* leave, leave quickly and quietly, sparing him the truth but unable to lie. And all along, he had blamed her in his mind, blamed her because of the money—and she was blameless, really; all along it was the man he had become, the man he had never known existed, the man the coward the weakling he had discovered and been appalled by for the first time just two days ago.

He knew that what had happened eleven years ago, the crime he had committed eleven years ago, had been the cause of it all, of what had happened to the man Steve Kilduff. He had been certain, so certain, that the incident had never affected him at all, when in reality it had been dragging him down by inexorable inches, destroying him, sapping his strength and his will and his initiative and his guts; latent guilt, hidden guilt, more deadly and more terrible than the kind which had been tearing Jim Conradin apart inside, because he had never known it was there, had thought he was free of it for those eleven long years. He had been living with guilt and with fear and he had never even so much as suspected it.

He knew all of these things, one after the other, like links in a chain being slowly drawn across his mind's eye; knew them to be true and factual without dwelling on them, as if his brain, a faulty computer, had somehow been reprogrammed, redirected. He knew them, and they were important, vital, feeding his desperate need to reach Duckblind Slough as quickly as possible, effectively blocking the doubts that lingered peripherally in his mind—doubts of the wisdom of this headlong flight, alone, without the police, into what was surely intended to be a trap; doubts of his own manhood, his ability to function, to make decisions in moments of crisis.

Andrea was all that mattered now.

And time was running out.

He passed through San Rafael, and his luck was holding. There had been no sign of a black and white Highway Patrol car. He controlled the big Pontiac—with its unpredictable power steering, its too-binding power brakes—as if the machine was a sports car built for speed and maneuverability and bad road conditions; deftly, with a skill born of purpose and desperation. Ahead, through the arc-sweeps of the rhythmic wiper blades, he could see one of the suspended freeway signs gleaming dully in the now-heavy rain: VALLEJO NAPA EXIT 1 MILE.

Black Point, Kilduff thought, Black Point. He couldn't use the county and private roads into Duckblind Slough—the only set of roads—because it was inevitably a trap and he would walk directly into it. If Andrea was still unharmed, what good could he do her dead, foolishly dead? His mind had not been calculating, weighing, coldly reasoning; he had allowed emotional reaction to rule. But it wasn't too late, not yet; the idea had grown and taken shape and it was an answer.

Maybe.

If there was enough time.

There had to be enough time . . .

He reached the Vallejo-Napa exit, just north of Ignacio. He left 101 east, oblivious to the red speedometer needle hovering near eighty now. When he had gone some eight miles by the odometer, he began to reduce his speed, looking for the Lakeville Highway turnoff. He saw it finally, the green and white freeway sign: PETALUMA and an arrow pointing due north, to his left.

He swung into the left-turn lane, waiting tensely for an opening in the westbound traffic. He saw an opportunity and took it, feeding gas to the Pontiac; the heavy rear end slewed a little on the rain-slippery macadam as he came onto the Lakeville Highway, but he fought the nose straight and bore down again on the accelerator. He was forced by the narrow expanse of the two-lane road to keep his speed under sixty, and it seemed as if time was at once, ambivalently, racing and sluggishly crawling. One mile passed, two, and finally three—and then he saw the black-lettered white sign, mounted on a tall silver-metal pole, looming against the dark morning sky:

Boat Launching Boat Rentals

TALBERT'S-ON-THE-RIVER

Winter Storage Live Bait

He touched the brake pedal, slowing, sweeping off Lakeville onto a wide, smooth asphalt parking area that fronted a weathered clapboard building with a railed and slant-roofed side porch. Beyond the building, there was a wide, steep concrete launching site with a chain winch at the top; and a long narrow T-dock with two Richfield gasoline pumps, extending some fifty feet into the blackly moving waters of the Petaluma River. There were boat slips on either side of the dock, between a slender, shell- and gravel-dotted beach and the parallel T-bar; small power boats and skiffs and rowboats, each bundled in heavy tarpaulin and protected by rubber or styrofoam floats, oscillated in the wind-swept swells. On the left, past a marsh growth of tule grass and cattails, were several storage sheds with corrugated roofs for larger boats.

Kilduff brought the Pontiac to a sharp halt, nose-up to the side of the weathered building. He threw open the door and ran across the wet asphalt, up onto the side porch. He pulled open the front door, the screen door behind it.

The interior was wide but not particularly deep, poorly lit, with a low beamed ceiling. The warped, unpainted walls were covered with shelves containing canned goods, fishing gear and equipment, boat repair and necessity items, dusty jars, bottles, tins of miscellany. A unit heater suspended above a short, bisecting wooden counter gave off waves of shimmering heat. There were two men at the counter, one behind it and one in front, both wearing heavy flannel shirts and faded blue Levis, the one behind the counter chewing on a long greenish-black cigar and sporting a thick dapple-gray mustache; they were arguing about the feasibility of dredging the river for the traffic of small freighters between Petaluma and the Port of San Francisco.

Kilduff let the screen door slam behind him, and both men turned to look at him. He went toward them, taking his wallet from his trouser pocket, fanning it open. His eyes were flashing and his mouth was grim.

He said, "Listen, I want to rent a skiff for a couple of hours, you can name your own price . . ."

The limping man had fashioned a sniper's nest.

A few yards from the wide clearing and the tan Volkswagen belonging to Orange's wife, just to the right of the entrance road, he had matted a section of cord grass and milkweed directly behind a thick clump of tall rushes. On either side, the tule grass grew densely to a height of three feet or more. Kneeling in the flattened area, hunkered low, he was certain that he could not be seen from the road or from the clearing.

Until it was too late.

He had been in the nest for perhaps fifteen minutes now. Immediately after he had called Orange from a motel-and-restaurant complex near Novato, he had returned here and parked the rented Mustang in a concealing grove of eucalyptus, well beyond the entrance to the second private road leading to Duckblind Slough. He had then walked back to this point, taking with him a tire iron from the Mustang's trunk; he had used that to snap the padlock on the wooden gate. Then he had swung the gate parallel to the road and walked the half-mile to the clearing, not hurrying particularly, despite the increasing velocity of the downpour, paying no heed to his sodden clothing—and set about constructing the sniper's nest. He had briefly debated waiting in the shack, but even though he knew almost exactly how long it would take Orange to reach Duckblind Slough from San Francisco, it would have been foolish to take even the remotest chance now, when it was almost over.

He shifted his weight, and his knees made wet slithering sounds on the matted grass. He had the .44 Ruger Magnum in his gloved right hand, pressed against his rib cage just below the left armpit. His palm was sweating inside the glove, and he could feel a certain expectant excitement building inside him. Just a few more minutes, he thought. Just a few more minutes and Orange will be dead, Orange will be dead, Red and Blue and Gray and Yellow and Green and Orange, all dead, all gone.

He wiped wetness from his face with the left sleeve of his overcoat, smiling a little now, thinking about how beautifully it had turned out. Orange had come home after all—no real matter where he had been all night—he had come home to answer his phone this morning. And he had suspected nothing wrong, nothing sinister; the news of his wife's death had sent him into shock, despite the fact they had separated—that had been apparent; no hesitations, no suspicions, he was on his way.

Beautiful, beautiful.

Of course, it was too bad about the woman. It really was, even though she was a whore like all the rest. She had fit so perfectly into the scheme of things, being here at the fishing shack—the perfect lever with which to lure Orange to Duckblind Slough. Without her, things might have been much more difficult. Yes, it was too bad about the woman.

He would have to kill her, nevertheless.

But not until he had made her scream for him the way he had made Alice-slut scream for him on Tuesday night.

It was only right, only fitting—his just reward—after all he had been through. But only after Orange was dead, only when it was all over. That was why he hadn't killed her before, that was why he had only tied her up without touching her, and put her in that closet.

The limping man looked at his wristwatch, listening to the rain falling on the morass, the wind howling, listening for the sound of an automobile. It wouldn't be long now, no it wouldn't be long now. Just a few more minutes, that was all.

And his finger caressed the Magnum's trigger as if it was the nipple on the breast of Orange's wife.

18

Steve Kilduff had almost reached Duckblind Slough before he realized that he had no weapon of any kind.

He sat drenched in the stern of a fourteen-foot, oak-hulled skiff—working the ten-horsepower Johnson outboard, fighting the craft through the roiling black water and through the cold, slanting rain—and told himself that he was a goddamned fool. He should have bought a gun, a knife, something, anything, at Talbert's, but the son of a bitch with the thick mustache hadn't wanted to rent him the skiff at all—"you're crazy to want to put out on the river in this weather, buddy"—and he had had to fabricate a story about his wife (Jesus!) shacking up with a friend in one of the sloughs and wanting to confront them in the act, so to speak. Mustache had smirked and winked at the other one and finally agreed for twenty-five dollars and a signed blank check as a deposit against damage, but Kilduff knew now that if he had tried to buy some kind of weapon the deal would have been flatly off, Mustache wouldn't have wanted any blood on his clean white hands. As it was, he had wasted fifteen minutes before getting the skiff out on the river, and all he had been thinking about was hurrying; time was growing more and more precious.

Still, there was the fact that he was completely unarmed. Even though he was coming in the back way, by water, with surprise in his favor, there was the chance that he would be seen; and if he was, he had no way to defend himself, he would be naked, a proverbial sitting duck in Duckblind Slough . . .

The shack?

Yes . . . the shack! There would be some kind of weapon there—a fish knife (he remembered having one) or at least a steak knife from the larder. If he could get to the shack, and inside, it might still be all right. He didn't think the killer would wait inside the cabin because there were, of course, no Marin County Sheriff's vehicles parked in the vicinity; realizing this, that it could arouse immediate suspicion—especially after the story he had told on the telephone—the killer would want to wait somewhere outside, possibly near the parking clearing, where he could make his move quickly and silently. That was the most logical place, the most logical decision.

But how could you really be sure about the reasoning of an insane mind?

And what about Andrea?

If she was all right, where did he have her? With him? In the shack? The shack seemed likely, because the killer wouldn't want to take the chance of her somehow giving warning from whatever concealment he had established on the marshland; yes, if she was alive she almost surely had to be in the shack. Then, if he could get there undetected, he could get her out, get her to the skiff, to safety.

If she was still alive . . .

Kilduff forced his mind away from the possibilities, from Andrea, forced it to key on what he was doing and what he was about to do. He peered through the driving rain and saw the entrance to the slough coming up on his right. He maneuvered the skiff in that direction, feeling, down the length of his body, the sharp jolts of the bottom slap-skipping across the rushing current. Once he had edged the craft into the narrow mouth, he began immediately to probe the left bank, looking for the small dock set into a miniature tule cove which belonged to Glen Preston—an investment broker from Santa Rosa who owned the nearer of the slough's three shacks. He would bring the skiff in there, he had decided, moor it to the dock and follow the shoreline on foot to his own cabin on the point; the thick marsh growth would conceal him from anyone at a distance inland—if he was careful.

He almost missed the cove, and he had to swing the skiff in a wide loop to bring it back, cutting the throttle as he did so. The craft settled and began to drift with the strong current, and he fed the Johnson more gas to bring it in close to the jerry-built structure; he cut back again, then goosed the throttle a little, cut back, and goosed a second time. The skiff's bow was almost touching the forward edge of the dock now. He gathered up the bow line, kicked the engine off, and gained his feet; he took two steps, using the fore seat as leverage for his jump to the dock. The skiff tilted dangerously in the roiling water, but he managed to land safely on the wooden planking. He wound the line around one of the vertical pilings and made it fast, pulling the skiff's bow up tightly against the edge of the dock to minimize as much as possible the strong threat of damage to the craft.

The wind lashed at his face, fanning his wet hair like a windsock, billowing the saturated material of his topcoat. The rain on his skin was like particles of ice. He turned to peer inland, and he could see Preston's cabin—a spectral gray blur—something more than one hundred yards distant. The path leading there was almost completely obliterated by the choking marsh growth. A natural drainage gulley, with three-foot densely grown banks, cut a jagged diagonal line to the cove from between Preston's shack and his own; its narrow expanse was swollen with muddy rainwater, which emptied into the slough ten feet beyond the dock. The cattails and tule grass grew down to the water's edge, and there was perhaps a foot of oozing black mud visible between the vegetation and the rain-lashed slough. Footing would be treacherous; you could easily become mired in that volatile muck if you weren't cautious. You had to use the thicker clumps of grass as stepping stones, and even then you took the chance that they weren't growing on mud islands or directly out of undetectable bog holes.

Kilduff drew a labored, tremulous breath, and stepped down off the dock, jumping over the narrow mouth of the drainage gulley. He began to make his way along the edge of the slough, leaning his body forward into the harsh north wind, his hands spread out from his sides, palms down, for balance in the stooped position. His street shoes, with their smooth rubber soles, slipped and skidded precariously on the wet grasses; it was as if he were attempting to make his way across ice. Almost inevitably, he lost his footing and went to his knees, his right leg splaying outward into the frigid slough, his hands clutching desperately at the vegetation to keep his body from sliding into the heaving water. He managed finally to regain his feet, to move forward again, slower now, eyes cast downward, measuring each step.

He came around a hump in the shoreline, and he could see his cabin then, squatting desolately with its odd, tired list, on the point. He paused, raising his body up slightly, searching the area immediately surrounding the shack. There was no sign of life, no movement save for the windswept marsh grasses. He turned his gaze inland, toward the clearing, but the rushes grew to heights of five and six feet—clumps of anise, of cats, almost as high—and he could detect nothing.

The shoreline bellied inland just ahead, and then drew outward sharply to form the point; at the center of the concavity, he would be less than a hundred yards from the clearing. If he had been correct as to the killer's approximate place of concealment, he would run the greatest risk of being seen when he passed along there. Well, all right, he told himself, just keep low, head down, let the growth hide you. Nice and slow, don't panic, don't blow your cool. All right, now, all right.

He started forward again.

The Marin County Civic Center—a sprawling, modernistic, turquoise-domed, gold-spired construction, distinctive in that it was the last creation of architect Frank Lloyd Wright—is located just north of San Rafael, directly off Highway 101 on San Pedro Road. Among other county and city offices, it houses the Marin County Sheriff's Department in a new annex on one of the upper levels.

Inspectors Commac and Flagg, having received a go-ahead from Chief of Detectives Boccalou, arrived at the Center a few minutes before ten. They passed beneath one of the tunnel archways to the rear parking facility, and then rode an escalator up to the annex. They were met there by a plainclothes investigator named Hank Arnstadt—a short, balding man with sad hound eyes—who would accompany them in a jurisdictional capacity.

After the amenities, Commac asked him, "What did the property check turn up, Hank?"

"Your subject owns a small fishing cabin in Duckblind Slough," Arnstadt said. "Tributary of the Petaluma River."

"How far is it from here?"

"Just north of Novato."

"Fifteen miles, maybe?"

"About that, right."

"How many roads in?"

"Just one," Arnstadt said. "Or if you'd rather, one set. One county and two private."

Commac nodded. "That's something, at least."

"Well, you can get there by water."

"In this weather?" Flagg said.

"Sure."

"I don't think we have to worry about that angle," Commac said.

"Do you want company on this?" Arnstadt asked.

Commac looked at Flagg. "What do you think, Pat?"

"We should be able to handle it."

"Yeah, I think so."

Arnstadt said, "I'll put a couple of units on stand-by, how's that?"

"Good enough."

"Are we ready, then?"

"Any time."

They used the unmarked sedan, Flagg driving. Arnstadt sat in the back. When they had pulled onto 101 northbound, he stared out through the rain-fogged side window and said in a morose way, "Lousy rain."

"Yeah," Commac agreed.

"I hope there's not going to be any trouble."

"So do we."

"How did he seem to you?"

"Kilduff, you mean?"

"Uh-huh."

"An average sort," Commac said. "Just a guy who made a bigger mistake than most when he was a kid."

"And got away with it for eleven years," Flagg put in. "Now that it's caught up with him, he doesn't know how to cope with it."

"Not a hardcase, then."

"No," Commac said.

"What about if he's backed into a corner?"

"Do you mean, would he fight?"

"Yeah."

Commac thought about it for a time. "No," he said finally. "No, I don't think he would."

There was someone inside the cabin.

Every nerve in Andrea Kilduff's small body seemed to contract, to become as thin and taut as piano wire, and she lay rigid in the darkness of the storage closet, her ears straining for a recurrence of the surreptitious, but nonetheless discernible, sounds she had heard only moments earlier: the muffled grate of the hinged window being slowly pulled outward; the scrape of hands, of feet, on the shack's outer wall and on the sill; the creak of the old, damp boarding as a certain weight settled gingerly on the floor inside.

But now she heard only silence.

Her heart seemed to be skipping every other beat within her chest;

it seemed as loud to her as a child's arhythmic thumping of a drum. Whoever had come in was standing in the room, outside the closet door, only a few feet from where she lay, standing and—what? Waiting? Listening, as she was listening? Who was it? The limping man? But if so, why had he come in through the window? Why hadn't he used the front door? And if it was him, what would he do now? Would he kill her? Would he shoot her, would he—?

Creak . . .

Oh God, he was moving now. She sucked in her breath silently, holding it, her eyes wide and staring upward.

Creak . . .

Footfalls, light and slow, coming closer, coming toward the closet door.

Creak . . .

He was right outside the door now, right outside, and almost immediately she heard the rattle of the lock in the hasp, and another rattling sound, different—keys?—and there was a soft clicking noise and the rattling of the lock against the hasp again, and then the door was being opened, slowly, slowly, and a shaft of bright gray light appeared, growing wider and wider, and a man's hand and arm, the arm encased in a muddied topcoat, a topcoat that looked—and in that moment she saw the man's face, unshaven, rain-streaked, saw his face, and her heart gave a surging leap, and warm stinging liquid came from nowhere and filled her eyes, so that she was looking at his face through a glistening film, like looking at someone under water—but it was his face.

Steve's face.

It was Steve.

He saw her at that same instant, and his eyes went wide and his lips parted, and there was a mixture of clear relief and a half-dozen other emotions mirrored plainly on his visage. He reached down and lifted her in his arms, strong arms, gentle, and she could smell the rain on him and the pungency of sodden wool and the warm, familiar maleness of him. He stood her on her feet, holding her tightly against him with his arms circling her body, his hands fumbling at the knot in the rough cloth gag, and then it was free and his name was on her lips as she kissed him, kissed his mouth and his eyes and his cheeks and the hollow of his throat, whimpering a little.

He nuzzled her hair, holding her, saying "Shh, baby, shh, it's all right, baby" very softly. After a time, tenderly, he moved her away from him and his eyes went to the shelves inside the closet, probing them left and right, pausing finally on a large green tackle box with chrome catches and a chrome handle. He stepped inside the closet, opening the box, taking from inside a long, bone-handled, wide-bladed fish knife with a double-edged, one-half-serrated point. He bent to cut the twine binding her ankles, and rose again to free her hands. He stepped back to put the knife into the pocket of his topcoat, and Andrea raised her partially numbed arms to encircle his neck. She pressed close to him again, clinging to him.

"Did he hurt you?" he said against her hair. "Did he touch you, honey?"

"No, no . . ."

"Where is he now?"

"He . . . left an hour or two ago, I don't know where he went."

"How long was he here?"

"Just since . . . this morning, after five . . . oh, Steve, who is he, who *is* that awful man?"

"I don't know, baby, I don't know."

"He wanted to know where you were," she said. "His eyes . . . his eyes were mad and he had a gun, Steve . . ."

His hands tensed on her back, but he said, "Shh, now, it's all right."

"Steve, how did you know I was here?" she asked suddenly. "How did you know . . . that man had been here? Steve, what is it, what's *happening?*"

He took her face in his hands gently and thumbed away the tears from beneath her eyes. He said, "There's no time to explain now. We have to get out of here. We have to hurry."

Andrea nodded, shivering, sensing the urgency in his voice, needing desperately to get away from Duckblind Slough, far away, to someplace warm and safe. She wasn't thinking clearly, not clearly at all; her mind was jumbled with questions and confused thoughts, with intensive fear. She allowed him to lead her across the room, beyond the Army cot to the unpainted wooden dresser. He took her wool jacket from its top and helped her on with it, and handed her the tweed slacks, which she had carefully folded there the night before. Obediently, she pulled the slacks up over her pajama bottoms and slid her feet into the suede flats at the foot of the cot. He took her hand, and his was at once very cold and very warm, solid and strong; he led her to the window and released her hand and took her waist and lifted her easily upward. She could feel the rain—frigid and somehow clammy on her skin—blowing in through the opened window, and she could see the turbid, wind-swirled slough, and the black-brown marshland beyond it. He lifted her over the sill, quickly, lowering her onto the slippery surface of the tar-papered floating dock. She stood leaning against the dripping planks of the cabin wall, feeling the dock sway beneath her, feeling a little dizzy, feeling the wind tug and lash at her skin, at her clothing, numbing her. And then Steve was beside her, taking her hand again, moving down off the dock to the mud and grass, telling her, "Walk where I do, honey, keep your head down and your body low, watch me."

She nodded reflexively, thinking: Steve, oh Steve, I'm so frightened, what's going to happen . . .

He squeezed her hand. "Here we go," he said.

19

Where was Orange?

Damn it, damn it, where the hell was Orange?

The limping man looked at his watch, and then leaned sideways to peer around the tall rushes, looking along the muddied expanse of the private road. Nothing, no sign of him. He should have been here by now, fifteen minutes ago. Had something gone wrong? Had he become suspicious at the last minute? Or maybe it was the rain, yes, traffic became snarled badly by the rain at times, that was probably it, Orange had just been delayed by the weather and he would be along any time now.

Hurry, Orange, hurry.

You can't keep death waiting.

The limping man leaned back against his upturned heels, letting his eyes drift eastward, toward the cabin. Across the bleak marshland, to the right of the structure, he could see the wind-frothed water of the slough; and he could see a marsh hawk, caught somehow in the deluge, fluttering erratically, very low over the width of the slough, seeking shelter; and he could see—

A *splash of color.*

Yellow, lemon-yellow.

Movement independent of the morass, of the elements.

Someone moving along the shoreline, away from the shack.

The muscles in the limping man's neck corded. Orange? Orange? No it was impossible damn damn damn how could it he couldn't have gotten past unless he had a boat a boat waiting and he had the woman he had come in sneaking and reached the shack and released the woman damn you Orange goddamn you to hell Orange . . .

He stumbled to his feet, taking the Magnum out from beneath his overcoat, and a tic had gotten up along his lower left jaw, pulling that side of his mouth down grotesquely, so that he seemed to be half-smiling, half-frowning, like a caricature of a comedy-tragedy theatrical mask. He stood there with his feet spread wide apart, staring through the rain at the shoreline, and he saw it again, the splash of color, the movement, and now the clear silhouettes of two figures humped over, holding hands, moving swiftly, recognizable.

Orange.

And the woman, his wife.

Blind rage welled inside the limping man, and there was no thought now of caution, of stealth; there was only the overpowering need to kill Orange, to end it, things had become complicated, no longer fitting precisely into a well-ordered progression, Orange had tricked him, fooled him, Orange had to die, die . . .

He lunged forward, starting to run, the Magnum extended in his hand, arm stiff, finger curling back on the trigger.

"Steve!"

Kilduff pulled up in the small belly of the shoreline, half turning as he heard Andrea cry out, and felt the sharp, frightened stab of her nails into the back of his hand. As he did so, his eyes lifted past her, lifted inland, and he saw what she had seen, saw the man running toward them, running crab-like through the wet, wavering vegetation, saw the stiffly horizontal arm with its black, manifest extension . . .

"Oh God, Steve, it's him, *it's him!*"

Her voice was laced with panic, and he felt a trapped fear rise in his own throat, a choking ball of it that made him feel as if he wanted to vomit. So close, they had been so close . . . He looked wildly about him, seeking a way out, an avenue of escape, but there was only the slough and the shack from which they had come and the dock with the waiting skiff and the sweeping expanse of the marshland. Four roads, and all of them were dead ends, box canyons, now that they had been seen. The slough was treacherous and Andrea couldn't swim; there was no protection and no weapon effective against a gun; they would make fine targets sitting in the skiff if they managed to reach the dock, and the chances of that were poor with the open shoreline; and the man, the killer, was running toward them across the fen. No way out, no way out . . .

He saw the roof of the shack belonging to Glen Preston, then, and an idea struck him, all at once, untenable perhaps, but there was nothing else, and he veered into the vegetation, pulling Andrea roughly behind him, moving diagonally toward the Preston cabin, moving toward a high thick cluster of sage. The wind blew stinging rain into his face, blurring his vision, and the tangled growth through which they were running tugged resistingly at his shoes and ankles. They plunged through the sage finally, beyond it; Kilduff felt something brush his face, whispering, cold, felt Andrea's hand almost slip from his, heard her cry out softly, and he stopped, pivoting, clutching at her, seizing her hand again, pulling her forward. They were some seventy-five yards from the cabin now, but the vegetation had begun to thin out, leaving only intermittent cover. Without breaking stride, he pulled Andrea to the left, through a circular patch of rushes, praying that the thick stalks—the cluster of sage—would hide them from the killer's view long enough, just long enough . . .

He saw the natural-drainage gulley fifteen yards distant, exactly where he had judged it to be, the banks grown densely—momentary concealment, momentary safety—and he slowed, allowing Andrea to rush into him, and when she had, he caught her around the waist and threw both of them forward, skidding through the grasses, over the bank, down the muddy sides and into the rushing, icy brown rainwater which flowed within the narrow spread. He held her tightly against him for a moment, fighting breath into his lungs, forcing himself calm. Then he drew apart from her, looking into her eyes, seeing them reflect the awful terror that grotesquely contorted her features. Her mouth worked convulsively, forming a silent scream, and he shook her roughly.

"Listen, Andrea," he said urgently, breathlessly, "get control of yourself, you've got to do what I tell you, now follow this gulley, it comes out by Preston's dock and there's a skiff tied up there, I don't think you'll be able to start the outboard, so just get inside and push off into the slough, let the current take you down to the river fork, you should be able to make it to shore there and find help."

She swallowed, digging her teeth into her lower lip hard enough to draw blood. "What . . . what are you going to do? Why can't we both—?"

"There's not enough time, he'll find us before long, now go—hurry!"

"Steve . . ."

"Damn it, do what I tell you, go, go!"

He shoved her away from him and she stumbled, almost falling, gain-ing her balance again, looking at him. "Go!" he said again, and she hesitated for an instant, but only for that long, turning abruptly and running as quickly as she was able through the muddy water, her hands clutching frantically at the reeds and cattails to maintain her footing.

He watched her for a moment to make sure she was obeying, and then he swiveled his body so that it was facing toward the cabin, Preston's cabin, his hands digging into the soft mire of the bank, gauging times and distances in his mind, guessing fatalistically that there hadn't been enough time, that he would run directly into the killer's arms, banishing the fear as rapidly as it had come, thinking: Decoy, decoy, move now, *move!* He scrambled up the bank, straightening into a low crouch as he gained the flat marsh ground, his eyes flashing in a wide rapid sweep through the wind-rain—and he saw the killer less than thirty yards away, running parallel to him in the opposite direction, toward the slough, saw him stop and jerk his body around as he spied his prey coming out of the gulley.

Run!

His legs churned on the wet, slippery turf, his eyes twisting frontally again, and he was gathering speed, running now in a low infantry zigzag, changing direction, changing pace, trying to blend as best he could with the surrounding terrain. The shack was sixty yards away, fifty, and he heard the first faint, distant, popgun-loud sound behind him, absorbed immediately by the howling gale, the bullet missing badly; heard a second report, absorbed, missing closer; heard a third shot—

At almost the same instant, he felt a sharp, stinging pain in the lower part of his back, just above the left kidney. That entire side went instantaneously numb, and he lost his balance, stumbling forward, putting out his right hand instinctively as he felt himself falling. I've been shot! he thought with a kind of awe, and he struck the ground solidly, jarringly, sliding on the slick wet earth, sliding behind a high growth of anise less than thirty yards from the northern side of the cabin. Breath burst from his lungs, and pinwheeling lights exploded in back of his eyes, fading rapidly after that first intense burst, fading into a series of large, cinereous dots that blended together to form a screen of murky darkness . . .

The limping man saw Orange fall, and a sudden premature exultancy seized hold of him. He pulled up, lowering his right arm, finger relaxing on the Magnum's trigger. He thought: Got him, I got him, he's dead, they're all dead, it's over, it's over!

But almost immediately, the methodical caution with which and by which he had functioned throughout the whole of it returned, and he knew he had to make sure, make certain, put a bullet squarely between Orange's eyes, no mistake. There would be enough time then to locate the woman—probably hiding where Orange had suddenly appeared, she wouldn't get away—and when he did he would make her scream for him and then he would kill her quickly and painlessly and mercifully; he had nothing against the woman after all . . .

He began to run toward the thick, fringed clump of anise behind which Orange had disappeared.

Andrea checked her flight, looking back over her shoulder, at the exact moment Steve came up out of the gulley and began to run. She froze, watching him lurch drunkenly across the open ground toward the Preston cabin until the high greenish-brown marsh grasses along the near bank of the drainage gulley blocked her vision—watching with the sudden realization that he was trying to draw the limping man away from *her* so that she could get away, escape . . .

Her gaze swiveled frenetically past the sparser growth on the opposite bank and across the morass to the north, and she saw the limping man racing toward the Preston cabin, his arm extended; saw the first indistinct orange flash from the large black gun in his hand, the second, the third; saw the limping man come to an abrupt halt, peering toward the spot where she had last seen her husband.

And her immediate reaction was: He's shot Steve, oh dear God, he's shot Steve!

She stood immobile as the limping man began to run again, vanishing momentarily as Steve had vanished. The turbulent rainwater swirled and eddied around her legs, and she was dimly aware that one of the suede flats had been pulled loose from her foot and carried off. She didn't know what to do. He had told her to get to the boat, get away from there and summon help, but what if he was badly hurt, maybe dying, maybe already— Oh no, no, he was all right, he had to be, he hadn't really been shot, this whole thing was so alien, so terrifying, she couldn't cope with it, what should she do, what should she do?

She tried to think, tried to reason, and after a moment she seemed to know the answer to her mute plea: Get help, yes, get the police, that was all she *could* do; she couldn't fight the limping man, she was only a woman alone. She had to get help, bring aid quickly, Steve was all right, he hadn't been shot, he would get away and she would bring help, she couldn't panic now, not now, she had to do what he had told her to do.

Andrea pivoted and began to rush once again toward the storm-flayed slough.

Kilduff shook his head violently, trying to clear away the gathering darkness in back of his eyes. He had no feeling in his left arm, and he knew that it was useless; he got his right hand under his chest, palm flat on the swampy ground, and lifted himself onto his knees, still shaking his head. Gray light—rain-blurred images—took away the darkness finally, and he could see again. He struggled upward, standing unsteadily just beyond the cluster of anise, chest heaving, looking toward the Preston cabin. Transitory cover, he thought, so futile, why does a man fight for every last second, every chance for another breath, when death is imminent?

He stumbled forward in a kind of awkward, spindle-legged run, not looking back, not daring to. Ahead he could see a narrow, squat, ramshackle structure—a woodshed—with shadowed gaps like missing teeth in its visible side, where the boarding had rotted or pulled away; it sat in a bayou-like quagmire void of any growth other than a few shocks of cord grass, ten yards from the near wall of the shack. Kilduff reached it, waiting for another bullet to slam into his back, tensing his muscles, girding himself for it as he ran; but he was past the shed, almost to the cabin, when the shot finally came, missing wide right, gouging wood splinters from the wall near the set of four stairs on the cabin's inland side. He threw himself forward reflexively, like a runner making a head-first dive into second base, skimming across and through the muddy pools, sending low wakes of spray outward on either side of him. He kept his head cradled against his good arm as he planed into the two-foot open space between the bottom of the block-raised cabin and the liquidy ground. He caught his forward momentum as he passed beneath the shack, twisting sideways, crawling through the fetid muck toward a vertical plywood section which served as a siding to the set of stairs. He crawled belly-down into the shadows there, wiped some of the slime from his eyes, and peered out.

He saw the killer come running in a limping gait one step past the woodshed, saw the black gun stretched forth in one hand. The limping man skidded to a halt there, legs spread wide, neck craned forward, seeing the slug-like furrow Kilduff had left through the quagmire. He remained standing there for a moment, indecisive, and then he took two quick steps backward, leaning his body back against the side wall of the shed, blending with the dwelling, no longer discernible.

Kilduff pulled the cold moist air hungrily into his lungs, still staring out at the shed, waiting, a growing weakness beginning to take command of his body, a frustrated helplessness permeating his mind. In that single moment of hesitation, he had glimpsed the limping man's face clearly through the pelting, stinging rain.

He didn't know him at all.

20

Andrea had come out of the drainage gulley and had climbed up onto the Preston dock—staring across to where the churning waters of the slough were hammering the skiff's bow against the upright piling—when she heard the single muffled gunshot.

She swung around, her eyes jerking upward along the straight, slender path leading to the cabin. She could see the shack above and through the swaying vegetation; and all at once, in a sequence of quick, film-like flashes: running figure, Steve, coming through the cleared area at the side of the cabin; thrown forward, flat dive; mud-spray obliterating him, swallowing him; second figure, stopping, gun plainly visible; moving again, backward, up against the wall of the small woodshed standing in the cleared area; no movement at all . . .

The same thoughts, the same fears, the same indecision that Andrea had experienced only a few moments earlier raced through her mind again. Had Steve been shot this time? Was he dead? Was he only hiding beneath the cabin? What should she do? This was so strange, so hallucinatory, there was no reason to any of this, no sense, it was as if she were trapped in a nightmarish world of instant replays.

Steve, Steve, what should I do—?

Suddenly, intuitively, she knew that if she obeyed his command, took the boat to get help, she would return to find a dead man—because this *was* real, starkly, terribly real.

He would die if she left Duckblind Slough.

Steve would die.

No!

No, he mustn't die! She had to help him, help him *now*, try to save him somehow; her eyes roamed wildly over the shoreline, searching for a weapon, anything, and she saw then the length of driftwood lying wedged into the mud just to the right of the dock, thick and gnarled, bark-free. She looked up at the cabin again—still no movement; the limping man was crouched at the side of the shed, peering raptly at the dwelling. I can circle up behind him, she thought, I can hit him over the head, knock him out, yes, I can do that—and before she could think any more about it, before she could examine the ultimate futility of her plan, she was jumping down off the dock, pulling the length of driftwood free of the mire, clasping it tightly in her fingers as she moved forward, going blindly, foolishly, suicidally, to help the man she loved . . .

The limping man stared fixedly at the spot where Orange had disappeared beneath the cabin, holding the Magnum against his right thigh, teeth clamped tightly, painfully together, as if trying to prevent the escape of the fury within his body.

Why won't he die? he thought. Why won't Orange *die?*

How many times do I have to kill him?

One more time, just one more. He'll be dead then, I'll make absolutely certain he's dead then. I'll kill him until he's dead. You won't get away, Orange, you won't escape . . .

Soft now. Careful. Does he have a weapon? Maybe yes and maybe no. A gun? No gun. He would have fired at me if he had a gun. No gun. Caution, though, can't be sure, can't go after him, have to wait, wait him out. I've waited ten years now, I can wait just a little while longer . . .

The knife!

The knife he had put into his overcoat pocket after cutting Andrea loose in the cabin, the fish knife!

The thought struck Kilduff all at once, and his hand groped feverishly at his mud-caked pocket. Had he somehow lost it in the fall when he'd been shot? In the dive beneath the cabin? His trembling fingers probed the sodden material of his overcoat and it was there, it was *there;* he traced the outline of the blade, the handle, and then he drew the pocket open and took the knife out and held it in his hand. A small chance, such a pitifully small chance.

But a *chance.*

Oh you Orange you're going to really die this time I'm really going to kill you this time you son of a bitch

He would have to rush him.

There was no other alternative.

Kilduff held the fish knife tightly in his right hand, its bone handle slick against his palm. He was still unable to see the limping man. Twenty yards to the woodshed; it could have been two thousand. There was pain now in the area above his kidney where the bullet had entered, muted toothache pain, and the weakness had bathed his body in hot, mucilaginous sweat, had sent tiny numbing needles into his good arm and into his legs.

I'm going to die, he thought suddenly. I'm going to die and I don't know why. I'll never know why and I'll never know who he is, this is just like . . . war. Yes, war, the mud and the rain and the cold and the waiting; this is how it was in Europe in 1945 and in Korea in 1953 and in Viet Nam in 1969—you don't really know your enemy and you don't really understand why you're there; oh God, this is all so terribly, horribly futile, so *useless*, this is war. And because it is, there is no other way except to kill or be killed, and you want so very desperately to live.

Andrea had had enough time to get away in the boat, but it could be an hour or more before she would be able to summon help. He wasn't sure he could keep from passing out for that length of time. And it was a certainty the limping man wouldn't wait very much longer. This was the time to attack, then, catch the enemy off guard, the element of surprise; he had to make the first move, the bold stroke, if he was going to have any kind of chance at all.

Now was the time.

Right now.

He got his left leg under him, digging into the soft mud with the toe of his shoe, leaning the upper portion of his body slightly forward, wiping sweat from his eyes with the back of his sleeve, dropping his arm to hold the knife low and in close to his body, ready now, tensing, trembling, knowing instinctively that he would never make it, knowing he had to try, counting five, four, three—

And he saw Andrea.

He saw her out of the corner of his eye, just leaving the tangled path which led to the dock, creeping through the grasses and through the slashing rain, holding a long piece of driftwood in both hands, looking frightened, looking determined. He knew instantly why she was there, what she was going to do, and he thought: You damned little fool, you crazy damned little fool! His eyes shifted toward the woodshed, but the limping man was still hidden; he hadn't seen her yet, no, because if he had he would have shot her, the instant he saw her he would kill her, Christ in heaven, why didn't she do what I told her to do, why?

Go back, Andrea, go back, go back!

But she kept coming, circling, thirty yards to the rear of the shed now, twenty-five, still coming, holding the length of driftwood clasped very tightly in her small hands, and he knew that the limping man would see her, hear her, any second now, twenty yards, any goddamned second now he would know she was there and he would kill her . . .

Kilduff shoved forward with his left foot, scrabbling on his hands and knees, out from beneath the concealing shelter of the shack's stairs, lifting himself onto his feet as he emerged into the pelting rain, holding the knife out in front of him commando-style, his mind completely blank, moving on instinct, and in that moment the limping man took a step away from the shed wall, into Kilduff's vision, turning his body as he saw or heard or sensed Andrea, not seeing Kilduff yet. The gun bucked in his hand, spurting fire like a deadly toy dragon, the sound of it terribly loud in Kilduff's ears, but Andrea was already falling when he fired, an almost comic pratfall as her feet sluiced out from beneath her on the treacherous ground. She screamed once, a high piercing sound which rose higher and higher as the muted reverberation of the gunshot died away, crescendoing, and Kilduff thought: *He's killed her, he's killed Andrea!* because he hadn't seen her slip, didn't know the bullet had passed harmlessly over her head, only heard her scream and saw her fall.

His eyes were locked on the limping man, and he hurtled forward through the sloshing mud, with his lips pulled snarling back from his teeth, the weakness forgotten, running in short, quick, sliding steps, the knife rigid in front of him, ready to rip through the flesh of the enemy half-turned away from him . . .

The limping man heard him coming.

The limping man heard him and pivoted toward him, bringing the gun around, and Kilduff could see his face—startled, the eyes like two tiny phosphorous pools—see it very close, less than ten feet away now. The limping man raised the gun, dodging down and to the left, away from the shed; he pulled the trigger, and the wide black bore seemed to discharge a billowing flame outward, flame and a noise as loud as a cannon firing next to his ear, and Kilduff went blind and he went deaf in that single instant, but the bullet passed high over his right shoulder. He plunged forward, trying to turn in the direction the limping man had turned, slashing upward with the knife, missing, missing, but his numbed left shoulder struck something soft and yielding and there was a small, gasping cough and he felt himself toppling forward, falling, falling onto the yielding surface—the limping man—and he tried to use the knife and found that he couldn't. As if in slow motion, then, they were rolling over and over, arms and legs locked, rolling through the oozing mud, and Kilduff felt it cling parasitically—a cold noxious flowing entity—to his clothes and to his skin. He could smell the man's breath, the breath of a satyr, thudding into his face in sharp staccato expulsions—

Suddenly, the limping man was gone.

Kilduff felt him jerk free, as if they had been exploded apart, one whole splitting into two halves, and he rolled again, coming up onto his knees, dimly able to see the limping man again and he too was kneeling, less than two feet away, staring back at Kilduff, the two of them with their arms hanging down at their sides, the two of them still with their weapons clenched in mud-fists, kneeling in the center of the brown quagmire just beyond the woodshed, gasping, frozen immobile there like two hideous, putrescent creatures risen from the slime for one long, long moment, seeming to wait one for the other, and Kilduff thought: *Andrea, oh God!*

With one final terrible effort of will, he brought the knife slashing upward and buried it almost to the hilt in the limping man's chest.

. . . And the limping man feels the knife, hot, white-hot, tearing through his flesh, and his mouth opens and air spews out in a heaving, agonized sigh. A grayness dims his vision momentarily, puts a gathering fog across the pupils of his eyes, and there is the distant sound of whining, vibrating turbines in his ears. He does not see or hear the Magnum fall from his nerveless fingers to make a soft, wet, ugly sound in the mud. He blinks once, twice, and finally the fog shreds and he is able to see Orange again, Orange releasing the handle of the knife, the muscles in his face relaxing, growing lax, his eyeballs rolling up in their sockets, falling backward, falling into the shallow brown bayou, lying still.

There is no pain; miraculously, there is no pain and the limping man looks down at the front of his slippery wet overcoat, at the mottled black and white handle of the knife protruding there, looks down at the fountain of blood bubbling out around it, his blood, covering the small exposed portion of the molten blade, painting the grip now, thick and flowing free, bright red rivers meandering down the muddied cloth; he watches them in mesmeric fascination, watches the rain dilute the brilliantine color of his blood, pale it, wash it away, watches new rivers forming, flowing red and thick again.

But there is no pain, there is only the sound of the turbines, growing louder now. He looks once again at Orange, lying still, and he thinks: He's dead Orange is really dead this time I've finally killed him! He tries to smile, for the fury and the rage are gone; but he has no control over his facial muscles and his expression remains frozen, mask-like. He begins to waver, slowly, as if he has suddenly become caught in a cross-current of the wind, and the fog obliterates his vision again, thicker now, thickly gray as his blood is thickly crimson.

It's over vengeance is mine Blue and Red and Gray and

The pain comes all at once, a searing, flashing tidal flood, erupting throughout his body, a holocaust of pain consuming the cells, the pumping arteries, the tissue and the membranes, destroying everything in its path. He cries out once, sharply, tormentedly, and then his brain ceases to function and he topples sideways, sprawling face-downward in the cold brown sucking mud . . .

Sounds.

The wind and the rain.

His name, screaming.

Men shouting, far away, coming closer.

All vague, all dream-like.

Kilduff teeters on the edge of consciousness, close to falling, soon to fall. He seems to be drifting within himself, an aimless drifting in descending, ever-diminishing circles, as if he has somehow become trapped inside a cone-like helix that will, when he reaches its tiny beckoning bottom, hurl him into a limitless black void. His eyes are closed, and he cannot open them; the rain is cold, pleasant, soothing on his fevered skin. He lies there, waiting for the void, drifting, drifting, and then he senses a weight fall beside him, hears the anguished sounds of near-hysterical weeping. Soft hands, tender hands, familiar hands lift his head from the mud, cradle it momentarily, lower it finally onto a pillowing, familiar softness.

Andrea's hands.

Andrea's softness.

Andrea you're alive, you're all right.

Oh God, thank you, God . . .

He tries to say the words he is thinking, but his throat refuses to work. The tender hands stroke his cheeks, and he tastes the salt-warmth of falling tears on his lips, Andrea's tears, and Andrea's voice is saying his name again, over and over and over, pleading with him not to die . . .

Running feet, pounding across the marsh grasses, through the puddles and through the mud. Panting breaths. A man's voice: "Jesus Christ!"

Another: "Pat, get back to the car. Radio for an ambulance."

Another: "They're both dead, Neal. Look at all the goddamned blood!"

The second: "What happened here? Ma'am, what happened here . . . ?"

He is nearing the bottom now, and the opening into the void has grown larger, grown wide. It waits for him, inviting, and he begins to drift faster and faster, reaching out for it, ready to embrace it. The sounds fade, diminish, until there is only a great, frightening silence.

And then he spins out of the cone-like helix, into blackness, into nothingness, into oblivion . . .

Epilogue
Friday

White on white.

White images superimposed on a white background.

Bright white light.

Belly-down on white softness, cheek resting on white softness.

The odor of antiseptic.

Faces—blurred faces, strange faces.

Pain in his back.

Binding constriction of adhesive tape.

Weakness.

Remembering.

"Andrea," he said.

"His wife," one of the blurred faces said.

"Andrea . . ."

"She's all right," another of the faces said. "She's right outside."

". . . see her . . ."

"Not now. Rest, now."

Faces fading. He tried to keep them in focus, but they faded and faded and finally they were gone, and the whiteness was gone and the softness and the light were gone.

He slept.

He awoke thirsty.

He was still lying on his stomach, still lying on the white softness. His vision was clear. He saw a white wall, white ceiling, white-linoleumed floor; white nightstand and a white-uniformed nurse sitting on one of three white metal chairs, reading a magazine.

He said, "Water."

The nurse stood up and looked down at him and felt his pulse. She smiled briefly and brought him a glass of water. He drank it, asked for another. The nurse let him have a little more, and then she left and he heard a door close. After a time, a doctor with black eyes and a cupid's-bow mouth came in and began to examine him.

"Do you have any pain?" the doctor asked.

"Yes, a little."

"That's understandable."

"How badly am I hurt?"

"You'll be all right."

"My wife—?"

"She's fine."

"Is she here?"

"Yes."

"Can I see her?"

"Not just now."

"I'd like to see her."

"There are . . . some men first."

"Oh," he said. "Yes."

"Do you feel up to talking to them now?"

"Yes, all right."

"I'll tell them."

His tongue felt swollen. "What hospital is this?"

"Novato General."

"And what day?"

"Friday."

"Morning?"

"Yes," the doctor said. "A little past nine."

"Almost twenty-four hours," he said.

"That's not unusual," the doctor said. "You were in surgery for five hours."

"I don't remember."

"No, you wouldn't."

The doctor left—and came back again.

With Inspectors Commac and Flagg.

And a man named Arnstadt.

And a male stenographer.

The first thing he asked them was: "Who was he?"

"His name was Marik," Commac said. "Felix Marik."

"Marik? Marik?"

"He was the driver of that Smithfield armored car you helped rob in 1959," Commac said.

"The driver," he said. "Marik, the driver."

"That's right," Flagg said. "You want to tell us about it now, Kilduff? The whole thing, from the beginning?"

He told it.

Once.

Twice.

And then he asked them if they knew why Marik had done it, why he'd wanted all of the hold-up men dead.

Commac said, "We got his name from his wallet and ran a check on him. It seems the Illinois police questioned him extensively after the robbery, although that fact wasn't made public. They thought he might have been involved—an inside man."

"Why?"

"Because he allowed the two of you to get as close to the armored car as you did," Flagg said. "But after a while, they figured it wasn't anything more than carelessness and gave him a clean bill. Smithfield fired him right after that. Negligence, according to the company statement."

Commac said, "He had a run of bad luck, bad to worse. Couldn't seem to hold a job. And then his wife left him, divorced him because of the notoriety involving the robbery. He went to Michigan and got a job finally as dock worker on Lake Erie."

"Two months later," Flagg continued, "a crate of heavy machinery fell out of a hoist netting and broke both his legs. He was in the hospital six months. That was the reason for the limp; tendons in the one leg never did heal right."

"Do you have any idea how he found out we were the ones?"

Flagg shook his head. "An obsession can make a shrewd investigator out of any man," he said. "We found a briefcase in his rented car out at Duckblind Slough. There were a series of folders on each one of you inside; he knew more about you than you know yourself, Kilduff. He was thorough and he was meticulous."

"Maybe something put him onto the fact that all six of you were recently discharged from the Bellevue Air Force Station at the time of the robbery," Commac said. "And that, as you said, all six of you remained in Illinois for three years after the robbery. Unusual for demobilized soldiers. We'll never know exactly how he did it."

"No, we'll never know."

And he thought: Marik had to have somebody to blame for what had happened to him, for all the bad luck. He couldn't admit to himself that he was the one responsible—that it was his own weaknesses, his own failings.

Like me.

Just like me.

They talked to him a while longer, and then the two of them—and Arnstadt and the male stenographer—left quietly and he was alone again.

The doctor again. "Do you want to rest now?"

"I'd like to see my wife."

"Yes," the doctor said, and went out.

He lay there looking at the wall. He turned his head on the pillow, and he could see the room's single window. The shade was up. He was in a ground-floor room, and he was able to see out into a small courtyard with two large, spreading oak trees.

It had stopped raining.

The sun was trying to come out.

He watched the wind blowing through the leaves of the oaks, and then the door opened and there were soft footsteps and Andrea was there, standing beside his bed, both her small hands clutching a black purse, wearing her wool jacket and a black skirt. She sat down on one of the white chairs, and he could see that her eyes were red and puffy and he knew that she had been crying, that she had not had any sleep the night before.

"Hi," she said.

"Hi," he said.

"How do you feel?"

"Fine," he said. "And you?"

"I'm all right."

"You . . . weren't hurt, were you?"

"No."

She folded her hands in her lap, and they looked at one another for a long time. Neither of them smiled. He found himself thinking back to that first day he had met her, in the café in Sugar Pine Valley, and he remembered how he had felt on that day, the thoughts which had entered his mind. He felt the same way now, as if he was seeing her for the first time: desire, tenderness, protectiveness, needing. His throat was very dry.

He said finally, "Do you know about it?"

"Yes, they told me."

"All of it?"

"Yes."

"I'm sorry, Andrea."

"So am I."

"I couldn't tell you about it," he said. "You know that, don't you?"

"I know that."

He was silent for a long moment; then, his eyes still locked with hers, he said, "I love you, Andrea. I tried to stop loving you, but I couldn't do it."

There was moisture in her eyes now, and a faint tremble to her lower lip. She nodded almost imperceptibly.

"Do you love me?"

"Do you have to ask?"

"No," he said. "But I need to hear you say it."

"I love you," she said.

"Andrea, I know why you left last Saturday."

She searched his face. "Yes, I think you do."

"I'm not the same man I was then."

"No, you're not."

He said, "What will you do now?"

"What do you mean?"

"Will you stay with me?"

"You know the answer to that."

"I need to hear you say it."

"I love you," she said. "I'll stay with you, I belong with you."

"It won't be easy for a while. It may never be easy again."

"Yes, I know."

"There'll be a full investigation," he said. "Even though the Statute of Limitations ran out on the robbery a long time ago. They told me that. They'll hold me until they find some way to prosecute me; and even if they can't find a way, there's a good chance the armored car's insurance company will bring a civil suit against me for restitution of the stolen money."

She was silent.

"I might go to prison," he said.

"Yes," she said.

"Even if I go free, there's going to be a lot of notoriety connected with all this."

"People forget," she said. "People forgive."

"It won't be easy," he said again.

She smiled for the first time, fleeting, sad. "It will be easier than it was in the past," she said. She rose from the chair and sat beside him on the bed and touched his hand.

He took her hand and squeezed it inside his own, looking up at her. They remained like that, not speaking, looking at one another under the bright fluorescent lights.

After a long time he said, "It's going to be all right, Andrea."

She kissed his forehead lightly.

And he said again, "It's going to be all right."